D1706687

ALSO AVAILABLE FROM POISON FANG BOOKS

BY Nicca Ray

Poetry
Back Seat Baby

BY CHRIS D.

FICTION
No Evil Star
Dragon Wheel Splendor and Other Love Stories of Violence
and Dread
Shallow Water
Mother's Worry
Volcano Girls
Tightrope on Fire

NON-FICTION
Gun and Sword: An Encyclopedia of Japanese Gangster Films,
1955–1980

YOU
USED
TO
KNOW
ME

Kris —
~~still~~ forever
soul sister

xo Nico

If you enjoy this book, tell someone about it

A Poison Fang Book

You Used to Know Me
© 2020 Michelle Cernuto (aka m.c. nuto)

Foreword
© 2020 Danny Bland

Cover/Design
© 2020   Chris Desjardins (pka Chris D.)

Front and back cover designs by C. D.

ISBN:9798550416921

First Poison Fang Books Edition, November 2020

Printed in the United States

10 9 8 7 6 5 4 3 2 1

You Used to Know Me

BY

m.c. nuto

FOREWORD

BY

Danny Bland

Preface by Chris D.

A Poison Fang Book

for
Todd Sampson
and the Las Vegas Punk Scene
of the 1980s

Preface

Writer m. c. nuto dives deep into what has become a touchstone
subgenre of both the *roman noir* and the ghost story. A tale told
by a narrator who is already dead. We, the readers, are aware
of this from the first page. The dead narrator – usually aware of
their state – is not uncommon in literature, from short fiction by
Edgar Alan Poe and Ambrose Bierce to more recent novels such
as Alice Sebold's *The Lovely Bones* and Muriel Sparks' *Hot-
house by the East River*. There have also been more films than
one might expect employing this convention. From the mainstream, award-winning noir, *Sunset Boulevard* to latter-day box
office horror smashes such as *The Sixth Sense* and *The Others*, to
countless cult films such as *An Occurrence at Owl Creek Bridge*
(the short by Robert Enrico from 1962), full-length features
Carnival of Souls, *Venus in Furs* (aka *Paroxismus* by Jess
Franco), *Jacob's Ladder*, *Alice or the Last Escapade* (an eerie
modern update of Lewis Carroll's *Alice in Wonderland* directed
by Claude Chabrol, 1977), et.al. The list could go on. Except
for *Sunset Boulevard*, most of these cinematic sagas feature
protagonists who – along with the audience – are not aware
they are deceased until the climax.

Many self-absorbed critics of both literature and cinema feel an already-dead narrator is a groan-inducing device, although why it should be so is a mystery to me. Perhaps because it is difficult to do it convincingly? Author m. c. nuto does not have that problem.

You Used to Know Me is a mash note from beyond the grave to a long lost Vegas. 1980s punk teen dysfunction, abusive high school cliques, traumatized ex-boyfriends, biker gang drug culture, unethical party monster doctors and former Elvis sidemen collide in a melancholic travelogue through a spiritual wasteland. The self-effacing murder victim gives us a matter-of-fact, blow-by-blow commentary as she haunts both her friends and her predator in a suburban, desert dystopia. Nuto's narrator has a casual, resigned familiarity with her new state of being, and her sometimes impossibly long run-on sentences enhance the disturbing nature of her fate. Her meticulous detailing of inconsequential teenage ephemera and first time crushes is given the same weight as the most horrific, blood-soaked trauma, and the effect is unnerving, harrowing and masterful.

Chris D.
Highland Park, CA
October, 2020

Foreword

Maybe there's an old cassette tape you put on late at night. You listen on a Walkman you hold on to for just such an occasion … and so as not to disturb your spouse. The music is not so much an acquired taste but something you had to be there for to understand. The tapes are battered and grimy with handwritten labels. Most of the bands had acronyms for names, letters whose meaning have long since escaped you. Your partner has more of a mainstream palate.

Maybe the family is asleep and you visit a slightly stale pack of smokes you've got hidden up on a shelf in the garage before retreating to your favorite backyard patio chair with a cold beer. You press play, and the sound is insanely loud and impossibly fast. Just like you were. Leaner, meaner and chock full of teenage indestructibility.

They say your past is just a shadow. It's a nice place to visit. You close your eyes, and it's a hyper-quick slideshow of blurry drives, bloody knuckles, handsy make-out sessions, white drugs, brown drugs, green drugs and the cheapest more-the-merrier alcohol you could find. Good clean American fun. Reckless, out-of-control teens will be reckless, out-of-control teens you think to yourself.

It is the culmination of these events that somehow formed the perhaps productive, sometimes happy, maybe upstanding citizen that sits staring up at the blue/grey smoke that drifts toward the stars in the suburban sky above you.

As a measure of defense, some memories are stored way back in the corner of your mind, under a dusty pile of fanzines, a box of Polaroids, ragged issues of Creem, whatever your flavor of poison to hoard. It's a moment, an indiscretion that rattles you and cuts through your nostalgic bliss. A shiver that causes you to sit up straight, crush out that cigarette and hold your head in your hands. We all have secrets.

This book is captivating from the jump and nervewracking for those of us who find comfort in knowing what direction we're heading. It is unpredictable, bold, raw and wickedly honest.

m.c. nuto's *You Used to Know Me* is that shiver down your spine.

Danny Bland
Seattle, WA
July, 2020

Introduction
and
Acknowledgements

This story is part memory and part vision, culled from dreams and nightmares, for the wild youth of the 2020s, from the wild youth of the 1980s.

I wrote it to describe something long-buried in my subconscious, woven into hallucinations born of survival and a desire for revenge.

And, a story of first love.

A missive for a blurry place and a time in my old hometown, for the kids of the black hole, who were always trying to dig out.

I thank my family - Ava, Sam, Carole, Tony, Paul, and all the ancestors.

I thank my friends Chris, Danny, Victor, Johnny, Dale, Stephanie, Kristin, Hollice, Dawn, Kathy, and Todd (may you rest in power).

I love you all to the stars and beyond, and back again.

- m. c. nuto
San Francisco, CA
July, 2020

Chapter 1
You Used to Know Me

Tonight they are going to blow up the Sahara hotel, the one
my dad worked in when I was a little girl and we lived near the
Las Vegas Strip. The Sahara is the resort my mom and brother
and I would walk a half block up to because they had a coffee
shop, and we would sometimes go and sit in the cool of the air
conditioning for a while, to eat dollar breakfast plates and kill
time while dad was out on tour with Elvis or The Rat Pack. Now
I am lurking here while the demo squad has stirred all the other
dead. Some of the dead are standing in the rooms, walking the
halls where the explosives are being rigged.

      I wander the first floor, and I pass by the lounge I wasn't
allowed into when I was a kid, and see an apparition of a man
in a chair with a crumbling, dusty, brain-encrusted black felt
fedora, oblivious to the absence of his lower jaw. A faded
woman in a mangy 50s stole, that is draped over the shoulders
of half of her skeleton is lying on the floor near the bar with
what appears to be her long-gone lover, both shot through the
places where their hearts once were. The bullethole goes
through the barely-anything-left fake gardenia corsage, pinned
to a decaying and beautiful gown, all three of them staring at

me absently, searchingly.

I pass by the showroom, where more than one spectral mob boss with a blown-off chunk of skull is sitting in between a couple of hollow, bled-out mistresses with leg bones shattered on the ground below the knee, forlornly yelling into the afterlife for someone *to get them a fucking cocktail already.*

I'm wandering the floors, first into a hotel room with spectral, empty pill bottles still on the mid-century side table next to the bed, where a woman still lies trapped and frozen in some heartbroken, long-ago memory of him, and then into one where a man is hanging in the closet with a note on the bed for his wife back at home, explaining how they'll have to move out of the house as the savings is done, and that he's truly sorry that he also gambled away the college fund.

In another room I pass by and stare into, three young men in paisley shirts and bell-bottom jeans are sitting cross-legged, with yellowed and empty syringes still on the floor in the middle of a circle made up of their limp carcasses, with two young women nearby on the bed, their long, still-growing hair trailing toward the floor like lovely vines, heads dangling over the sides of the mattress.

Everyone in the rooms sense something is about to happen as I pass by, but they don't understand why I'm leering at them. They've seen me here before, but this is a new energy from me, as if I'm walking by one final time, saying goodbye. I am, because this is what I do for fun now. I walk the halls of the resorts again, before I ride the exploding buildings down into the fragments of concrete and drywall and I-beams and mattresses, side tables, bathtubs, toilets, glass and curtains. My after-death carnival thrill ride.

I lurk at all the old hotels now, not just the Sahara, and make certain to stop in one last time as they prepare them for demolition and implosion. I walk the halls as the workers lay the dynamite and everything else that will destroy these monuments to my childhood.

I walk the lined paths of the explosives with which they've traced the hallways of the floors. I see all the other spirits lurking in the rooms they died in, not aware they are about to get it. I go up on the roofs of the high rises and plummet into the tumble of the buildings, a sensation that feels like going under the waves of a concrete and iron ocean. My non-body finds it exhilarating.

I decide to haunt Jenny now that it's very late and very early. A tiny bit of light is starting to glow in the eastern sky, as I wander out of the rubble of the Sahara. I find her in a strip club behind the neon of the Strip, where she has a job dancing at the crustiest club on Industrial Drive. She's still alive, both top-less and bottomless, and yet I can only see the huge empty void of her absentee soul. She's as thin as the pole she's flailing her skinny legs around. I watch closely, unseen, from the stage. I am deeply saddened. Not by her nudity, but by her lack of life-force and purpose. There's a lone man at a slot machine, and the house band covers Pablo Cruise as a long-haired shirtless singer croons something about a place in the sun. She half-asses a toss of her dry yellow hair to the beat and grinds her pelvis toward the pitch black stage as the obscenely cheerful chorus gets mauled. Fuck this song, I think, watching her grind.

I am dead in a such a way that I can hear other voices in my head as well as my own voice, and sometimes I can't tell if I have a separate life instinct when I'm in proximity to someone I love or once loved. As I watch her, I feel numb, druggy, heavy, and anything but sexual. I hear a voice in my head wondering about the cost of the drugs after my shift...no one seems to be tipping tonight. I am without any normal visible connection to the living, yet my lack of physical body seems to allow me to penetrate prior temporal boundaries of space and time and the normal boundaries of consciousness. I don't know how I can know so well what they are thinking or feeling.

When I was alive, I didn't think much about ghosts except for maybe on Halloween when I was a kid but, now that I am dead, I reckon I must be one, and yet I feel most of the time as if I'm trying to convince myself of the situation. I am also not sure I believe in a separate me anymore, because I feel so merged with everyone I truly loved. I am still here, still tethered to the living, to living people like Jenny, but at the same time, I am me. I wonder if I am fractal of infinite consciousness like the theory I read about in that Timothy Leary book I checked out from the library in high school. I also wonder if I'm another lost soul doomed to wander the ghost highway, the kind of soul Hank Williams sung about in those old songs my mom loved.

My former body resides in six feet of hard dirt about thirty paces away from the tire tracks near the second fork on the road that takes you out to the cliffs at Lake Mead. It's a nasty stretch, and it's mainly driven by kids in shitty cars who want to smoke weed and drink and jump off the twenty-five-foot high embankment that lines the western side canyon area of the lake. We used to go out there, strip off our flip-flops, shorts and tank tops, and take a running leap into about thirty feet of dirty water. Middle-aged guys would troll in their middle-aged guy boats for underage cliff-jumping girls, girls they could convince to sit on their middle-aged laps and ride out with them to Hoover Dam. Sometimes those innocent young cliff-jumping girls would find themselves in deep trouble out there in the deep water near the Dam. But that's not how I died.

Frequently I hang out where my body lies, mainly because, I guess, that's home now. My buried body is encircled with roots from the mesquite and creosote, and the roots pull my still-growing hair in crazy directions, hair that looks to me like a horrifying but hilarious parody of a late 70s country-pop singer. It's country-singer big, but it's in every direction at once. It sits high around my skull in a way that I think would have impressed my teenage goth-punk rock friends, some of whom still miss me and think about me.

I wish I could show it to them. The ones that aren't dead like I am have jobs, kids, recovery programs, car payments, mortgages, thinning hair and thickening waistlines. I imagine us sitting on my unmarked grave, sharing stories about old times, me a dug-up skeleton with graveyard country-singer hair and them sitting on the roofs of their parked mini-vans with the child seats in the back, shooting the shit about the old days. We could go out walkin', after midnight, out on the highway.

Before I died, I wore boots from the army-navy store and listened to loud punk records that I bought at the one record shop in the whole town that sold what I needed to hear. Reagan was president, and we were angry about that, Reagan and his encroaching class war and fascism and his AIDS denial and racism. We had DIY bands, warehouses filled with loud music we played for each other, homemade haircuts done with electric shavers, t-shirts with offensive slogans, thick-soled creepers, and anything weird and old from the plentiful thrift stores.

My memories didn't die when my body did, and they often appear as visions while I am visiting the living. For all the death I'm surrounded by and able to see as I stalk the dying casinos and my friends and grave site, I might as well be simultaneously getting up in the morning for school, sitting in class thinking about him, taking the bus back to the motel we were staying in right before I disappeared, and eating the leftovers he would bring me back from his job as a busboy at the Peppemill Restaurant and Bar. I remember us waking up in the early evening to go to see a band play a warehouse show at our venue, Room 13.

Past and present blur and coexist in my mind without boundaries. When I hang around my friends, I feel the same emotions I always did. I'm not moaning and rattling chains and floating in a white dress around the hallways of my loved ones, trying to scare them like ghosts in the movies. While I kind of like the idea, I don't crawl out of their televisions in some dark

gray formless mass, or try to get at them to suck out their souls.
Sometimes I'll go to them to visit at their jobs or at their homes,
but only if I know they're not in the shower or doing something
private that they don't want me to see. I can feel that they really
do feel me, too. I want them to see me. I wish they could see me.
They used to know me.

While it was much harder to know how someone felt
about me when I was alive, now I really know how someone
I love feels when I'm with them. Todd doesn't cry as much
anymore like when I first went away, so I don't feel his despair
and desire to join me as much as I did when I first vanished,
even though he stayed drunk or high through most of my
disappearance and didn't pay a whole lot of attention to himself
or his state of mind, until they never found my body.

Most of my friends don't know me anymore except for
Todd when he's drunk or high. Sometimes he sees me curled
beside him in bed when he wakes in the middle of a dope sleep
after a show. He knows an energy that has to be me is touching
his chest for his heartbeat in the middle of the night as he startles
himself up with another snore that sounds like a death rattle. I
rarely got drunk or high when I was alive, and I almost always
did the watching over when other people got high. I was always
the watcher of my sleeping friends, curled up next to them. I
often laid next to him this way when we were alive and had rock
and roll high school in fifteen dollar motels on The Strip. He'd
be high, and I stayed awake the same way so I could check his
heartbeat in regular intervals. Sometimes I'd fall into an acciden-
tal nap, but I was always ready when it was time to go see bands
at Room 13, even it if meant going in my long t-shirt and torn
fishnets and messy nap hair – he was always in a rush.

Now I sit next to him on the beds where I can find him,
and I ghost-touch his forehead and feel his chest. Sometimes he
goes to the cheap motel we used to stay at, when his graveyard
shift as a chef at the 4 star restaurant on the Strip is over. On the
last night of the work week, as he smokes tar to come down from

another day-into-night cocaine binge, I'll find him and whisper in his ear for to him to wake up wake up wake up, you can't join me here.

As he wakes, sometimes he'll see me and smile and fall back into a tomb sleep, reaching out to encircle not-me with his arms. Sometimes I will lie there next to him to listen, with my dead but still- listening ears for his heartbeat, or I will stare endlessly with my not-blinking eyes at the neon signs from the motel windows. I'll be there when he dreams about us sitting in the front seat of the van as we accidentally drive into another flash flood and stall out and, in the dream, he will pull me back to the bench seat to have sex, and I'll join him in the dream and be with him until the dream water flows out of the storm drains and into the dry washes and down to the lake.

Chapter 2
Boredom is the Reason

Multitudes of past and present exist side by side, and I have nothing but time, yet there is also no time. I often visit our childhood homes, and I can see what was, as well as what is. I sometimes forget there are new people living there now, and they occasionally startle me. I also see other spirits like me in these houses, people wandering around, dead like me. But the dead don't startle me.

I am most fond of my childhood bedroom and my grandparents' living room. In my mind, the old photographs on the walls of our houses cover the new photographs on them, the pool table sits in the middle of a new dining room set, and their couch is superimposed over our old couch. My fingers trace the bulletholes that went through the glass and into the black-and-white photos on the walls that hang over the new framed color photos of other families. I see the bullethole that went through my grandmother's beautiful marble-white face, a perfect circle bore into the space between her eyebrows from the night they were held at gunpoint by the drug dealers – the night the framed photographs were shot, but she was not.

My desire to return to these houses is an instinct. I find myself very strangely standing around in these houses because, at the times when it's darkest, those are the times that I feel like things tend to go very wrong. I hover over the bed of the girl who sleeps in my old room, and I stand over her in vigil. She doesn't know me, but I believe I am able to keep other spirits, living and dead, away from that room because I intend to scare any visitors who would do her harm. I am very relieved that I never have to, but I do it anyway. She's not yet twelve. Her bed is in the same place mine was.

Sometimes I wait around on my old schoolyard or down at the 7-11 and watch for the police and the people who capture the footage for the television series, *Cops*. This is now a neighborhood where they get a lot of good scenes to edit into the Las Vegas version of the police entertainment TV show. When the on-camera police come to bust the perps, the people shooting video and I will often be with the victims that they don't show because sometimes the paramedics aren't there yet, but the cops are. Sometimes I try to be near the people who do stupid, non-violent crimes while high, because they are getting arrested and sometimes don't even know what they did. I watch the skies for the helicopters that come at night to search for the people who are hiding from their dumb, sometimes violent crimes.

I hang around the park where I first barely got high on shitty weak pot, and I wait for the helicopter that followed us home that night with its scanning spotlight and frightening, chopping loudness. It never comes for me now that I'm dead, but it comes for others who I sit with as they get stoned, as I watch us getting high beside them. I float over the path to the junior high, where we were chased by the same half-naked man for weeks through the desert. I watch him in his car with the windows down, pants off, no underwear, his car bumping over rough desert and driving over cactus, chasing me and my friends but never catching us, because you can't really drive a car through unpaved desert very well or very fast, a fact that never

seemed to deter him in his pursuit of our young bodies. I
hover in the spot where we had bonfires, the stacks of wooden
pallets fifteen feet high. I float high up over the fires and the
dumb drunk kids, the ones who burn the bottoms of their army
boots and converse trying to jump the flames when the fire gets
low.

I go up to the old mining caves, where the kids will
climb through them at night like we did, using Bic lighters to get
from one side of the interior of the mountain to the other side.
They crawl next to my visions of us, over the interior, collapsed
sections of mine, sometimes scaling small hills within dark
tunnels to get to the side that overlooks the valley floor. We all
sit in the gravel on that side that faces downtown, side by side,
specters of the past next to the present, enjoying the flickering of
the lights of the neon city below.

I am there as a teenaged girl falls asleep by the bonfire
in front of the cave like I did once, and there beside her on the
wooden pallet, I see myself asleep, too. as a young man attempts
to rape me. I wake my former self up as he tries to undo my
pants, and I push him with my ghost body and my real legs
into the fading bonfire. Afterward, a boy in the backseat on the
ride home throws up out the shared car window of the Dodge
Charger, and I see some of it fly into my long hair as I sit in the
front seat with my friends, and he misses the window, as the car
drives phantasm-like, through another car, as it leaves the
bonfire.

I go out to the site of the Mint 400 race, to watch the new
model vehicles racing alongside, or fading into and out of, the
old rugged dune buggies from the era of my childhood. I gaze
upon us, asleep in our tents next to them in their tents. I drift
near the pond and look at them as we all swim through time and
space in the muddy hot springs, picking up leeches the size of a
baby toe on our shins.

I stare at us being offered cocaine in custom vans in the nearby dunes with men old enough to be our fathers. I drive over the dirtbags, still giving high school kids meth and beer and letting them go out for miles on their off-road bikes, and I leer at my uncle as he accidentally drives over his friend's head after he falls out in the dunes, while balloon-tire trucks drive down the real embankment. I hang over my uncle's truck as they drive the man to the hospital, everyone high and paranoid, while the man with the crushed head moans, still alive, and on the same highway the newer model trucks speed by, side by side.

Chapter 3
American Youth Report

In 1969, my dad got a job at the International Hotel to work in the TCB Band, the band that backed Elvis. TCB is short for Taking Care of Business, a phrase Elvis used as a mantra. They worked The King hard, and so he needed uppers for work and to keep his weight down, and downers to sleep and push his anxiety and heartbreak away. They gave him so many he was high as a kite for years, living like a ghost before he was even dead.

Before we moved to Las Vegas permanently, we would travel from gig to gig in a 1961 white Lincoln Continental with suicide doors, white leather seats and a blood-red leather interior. The first bedroom I can recall was the big leather backseat of that smooth-riding American car. I loved the sound of the whitewalls rolling on the asphalt a foot below my head as I napped on the seat or played the Tupperware lid exchange game on the back-seat floor with my older brother. At night, before going to sleep, I watched the stars float by on the way to the next gig, in the velvet sky outside the window, which looked like heaven. My dad played trombone in touring acts, with Sinatra, Perez Prado, or with whatever came up.

Before The International, the circuit he did was mostly between Los Angeles, where I was born and where we lived, four of us in a series of one-bedroom apartments, and Las Vegas, Reno or Tahoe. Sometimes he'd get hired to travel overseas for tours and would be away for weeks. We'd stay in Vegas for short chunks of time before we settled there permanently. We lived off and on in a tiny 50's dingbat style apartment complex on Sahara Avenue, a two-minute walk to Las Vegas Boulevard, also known as the Strip. My mom, my brother and I would stay behind during the tours my dad did. We would walk to the Strip, take the bus downtown to Fremont Street where there was a Woolworth's, and go to the Foxy Dog or Golden Gate Diner for lunch, and try to keep ourselves amused. Glitter Gulch was what we called Fremont Street before it was covered up with a big TV screen canopy. We didn't have a shopping mall then. We had the Foxy Dog, Woolworth's, neon Vegas Sal waving hello, and the bus.

My favorite casino sign on the Strip was The Stardust. I loved walking down by it at night and looking at the colors shifting – purple to blue to light blue. I loved the idea of stardust coating all of us, blanketing us with outer space, visions of the endless night sky floating by the car window dancing in my little kid head. Sometimes we'd go inside the casinos for cool air and see celebrities like Joey Heatherton walking in for her shift in the showroom.

I remember asking my mom if Ms. Heatherton was a hooker, as she strutted by in her sequined leotard and fishnets. Mom quickly shushed me, seeming surprised that I knew the word. But even she knew they would prowl outside the casinos and say provocative things to us, especially when my dad was with us in his work tuxedo. Sometimes on the corners near our apartment, they would open their fur coats to show their nude bodies to cars driving by, including ours if my dad was driving.

I like thinking about Elvis, remembering how he was a good boss to my dad, and how the TCB band members and other lounge musicians on the Vegas circuit were dad's work friends. When we finally settled in and moved out of the apartment on Sahara, we got a ranch-style tract home out in the desert in the middle of actual nowhere.

My brother Jack, older than me by two years, made friends with all the neighbor boys. The desert was vast and open and, finally, our two-bedroom house was nice, and we had little beds instead of army cots, and bikes to ride in the street. My dad put down sod in the yard around the entire house, and my mom planted morning glories and zinnias.

We had a cinder block wall that went the length of the block behind the houses and, when we first moved in, there were no divider fences between homes so the kids had the run of everyone else's backyards. Behind the cinder block wall, there was a big old tree that had been there for years. Someone's father built a fort in that tree, and we spent hours in it, holding intense surface-to-air dirt clod wars or reading comic books.

I flash to a vision of the Gila monster that climbed up and sat for a while on my lap up in the tree fort, viewing my child self lightly touching it before it crawled away and down out of the tree. My brother, who was five-and-a-half to my four-years-old at the time, noticed it and decided that I was going to die on the spot from a venomous bite. He knew it was a poisonous lizard native to the Southwest because he had a Boy Scout field guide and could read. I was illiterate and blissfully unaware.

The neighbor boys ran in a pack, and I would run with them and my brother, even though I was one of the younger kids. I'd do a lot of watching because I was too young to assist with the perpetrating of horrors around the neighborhood. Some of the boys had slingshots, and I'd stand around while they shot out the windows of the model homes, or took out streetlights at dusk because dusk was curfew and streetlights made them mad. Some of the boys would dig up fire ant hills and put them in buckets, and throw grasshoppers in to watch them be bitten by armies and eaten half-alive, or they would make us little kids lie down under their homemade wooden ramps, and see how many of us they could jump over on their one-speed bikes with banana seats and ape hangers.

Some neighbors would be fancy enough to dig swimming pools. We'd entertain ourselves for hours once they were filled with water, by sneaking down to their yard and throwing things in from behind the cinder block walls, listening for the plop of the dirt and rocks and then running away before they called the police.

I remember our neighbor Deenie, and how much I liked her. She was a teenager, wore cutoffs and had long hair, and seemed to me to be the coolest person that had ever lived. We sang along to a 45 of "Billy Don't Be a Hero" on her record player – the saddest song I had ever heard, and she told me she cried herself to sleep because her boyfriend was cheating on her with other girls at her high school. She liked to comb my hair and hold my hand and take me on walks around the neighborhood like a puppy. She'd feed me slices of plastic-wrapped processed cheese from their fridge, and we'd watch game shows on TV. When her parents dug out the yard for a pool, they found a skeleton in the ground. I was there the day the backhoe dug it up. The skull was intact, and it tumbled out of the digger, and Deenie and I saw it fall onto the pile of rubble from the sliding glass door in the living room where we were watching *The Price is Right*.

I am also drawn into pawn shops, junk stores, and thrift stores. I love being around the remains of what were once the items of physical lives. Sometimes I find our old things, like an afghan crocheted by my great grandmother, or an heirloom serving plate brought from the old country, passed down through five generations. At the moment, I'm drifting around the second-hand store on Boulder Highway near the turnoff to Lake Mead, the one closest to our old house, looking at photo albums that belonged to my family.

There's one that mostly has pages from 1972, the year my parents had another boy child, a sweet little baby named Saul. In the photos you can tell that Vegas was growing exponentially – there are snapshots of the grade school across the street from our house where we all went to school. When my parents were expecting my younger brother, Saul, we moved across the school from our first house, and my dad's parents moved into the house my dad had bought with his Elvis money.

My dad made the new house into a four-bedroom by converting the garage into another large bedroom, so now we all had our own rooms. My grandparents also brought an extended family of Italian relations from back east with them to Las Vegas when they moved.

There are photos of my dad's parents from when they first moved from Los Angeles to Las Vegas and into our old house, photos of my dad's father when he got a job as a security guard at the showroom where Elvis performed, working his way up to the chief of security in a few years. During those years, grandpa worked his Sicilian mafia connections and expanded them to a minor grift, wherein he would sell used, decommissioned TVs from Vegas hotel rooms to Teamsters who would resell them at a markup.

In the photos of my dad's family, the mixture of Northern Italian and Sicilian immigrants are shown celebrating holidays and standing proudly next to large, well-made American cars or newly purchased homes, as they moved around the country in large clusters. There are photos from Little Italy in early-1900s New York, then photos from Johnstown, Pennsylvania where they worked in slaughterhouses and steel mills, doing the jobs the other immigrants would not do.

From the 1950s, there are shots of the big move to Los Angeles, and many photos of my paternal grandmother, a mid-

century Italian-American dream girl. There are photos of
her with father Elea, a stone mason and her mother, my nonna
Orsola, whose immigration papers listed her simply as 'peasant.'
They both moved from Belluno, Italy because of war and
famine. My grandmother is so dear in the photos with her many
siblings. As one of the oldest, her fortitude and strength of
character leapt off the pages to me. I find myself
desperately wishing that I could find her in my afterlife as I
look at her photos. In pictures of grandma as a teenager right
after they made the basement red wine, in her dress slip and
stained feet and leather moccasins with no socks. There's more
of her and her four sisters baking bread, necessities that their
family sold during the Depression to feed their large family.
There are a few of her as a new mother, in chic dark lipstick and
a smart 40s suit, holding my baby father.

She's wearing the same smart suit and lipstick in photos
with my grandpa in his army uniform, at the local courthouse
after they eloped and he was stationed briefly in Idaho during
WW2. There are photos of the two of them in Los Angeles where
she got a promotion, having kept her job with the telephone
company all the way from the east coast to the west coast, and
a few of my grandfather in front of the company he worked for
that made rocket engines. My dad's parents are shown putting in
a pool, planting palm trees and Italian cypress in the front yard,
and the family watching TV in front of kidney-shaped tables in
the living room of their modern looking 50s tract home.

There are photos of their poodle named King and my dad
and his two sisters, all dressed like child stars. There are ones of
my grandma and grandpa from when they would visit Las Vegas
to gamble and stay in the resorts, just a short drive from LA on
Interstate 15. There's a whole album from 60s and early 70s Las
Vegas. The first few pages are of showrooms and lounges in Las
Vegas, a lot of my handsome young dad before he had kids,
posing with his trombone and King, the poodle, in his new job
as a union musician in the showroom circuit. The last few pages
have some of my grandpa with low-level mob connections, and

one of him and my grandma with Frank Sinatra some
seedy looking capos.

There are a lot of shots in my grandparents' home,
after they moved to Las Vegas and brought their whole extended
family, showing us kids how to use the pool table at my grand-
parent's house in Vegas, and many with my uncle Frankie at
the wet bar in the living room. There's some of grandpa at
the piano with the poster-sized blown up black-and-white of
Sinatra and the capos framed on the wall in the background, or
my grandfather at work smiling and showing off one of the fake,
augraphed, blue polyester Elvis scarves they used to sell to the
women lined up outside the showroom.

There's a few of him holding a martini shaker, another
one with a family poker game in the back. There's one of a table
filled with holiday food, notably the ever-present pan of lasagna
and soft bread, and the smiling great nonnas, proudly displaying
the fruits of their kitchen labor.

The pages of pictures from our first neighborhood
illustrate the youth takeover, as it started filling up with young
families and the once abundant desert started turning into
houses. My mom painstakingly added all the classroom and
headshot photos of all our years of public school to fill almost
an entire album, and then there are a few pages of photos of
neighbor parents – my best friend's Cuban dad in his flight suit,
who worked at Nellis Air Force Base. There's another page of
my friend's mom posing in her showgirl outfit, representing a
uniform of the factory town life. More snapshots of me and my
brothers with the kids from Havana who lived on the east side of
our house, and the other neighbors on the west side, a Mormon
family with five kids whom I can remember babysitting when I
was twelve. There are a few photos of the pantomime concerts
we put on with our friends, with cheap guitars and kiddie drum
sets in that converted garage, lip-synching along to records like
Mae West's "Wild, Wild West" at 33rpm.

I gaze at a school picture of my first boyfriend, a
neighbor kid I played basketball with on the playground every
afternoon. He taught me to shoot baskets, one after another.
We fell in love over our shared love of the Harlem Globetrot-
ters. There's a picture of my brother, Jack, with his best friend,
Terry, from up the street, whose parents divorced the year Jack
and Terry made friends. There's one of Terry's mom holding him
in her arms, the mom who was a showgirl in the Lido de Paris at
the Stardust and, because she was getting divorced, Terry would
stay with us for the first half of the night while she was at work.

Terry's mom would come in the side door of the garage
bedroom where we all slept and pick him up. In this image, she's
wearing her spangles, two-inch eyelashes, nude hose and showgirl shoes, but it looks like she's going to work because she has
her feather headpiece holder on with an unzipped windbreaker
over her skimpy outfit. As a child, she looked to me like a cross
between a hooker and a figure skater. She showed me how she
had to walk downstairs looking straight ahead, without looking
down at her feet, a showgirl trick of the trade. My dad's father
proudly told me when I was a girl that he hoped someday I
would be a showgirl at the Lido, because I was tall and scrawny
and flat-chested. I'm looking at the photos we took goofing off
on the golf course in the neighborhood where Howard Hughes
lived and was reported to have kept his urine and fingernail
clippings in Mason jars, a notable fact my mom always pointed
out when we drove by the window that faced the street side that
was reported to have been his bedroom. There are more shots
of Elvis performing in the showroom, with my dad's head in
the horn section behind him, and more than a few of my dad in
an orchestra backing Sinatra at Caesars Palace. There are a few
pages of dad with his rock band at his second-shift gig, working
the late-late show at the Pussycat-a-Go-Go.

I've decided that maybe my brother accidentally dumped
these albums here when he cleared out our old house for my
parents when they left Las Vegas and moved to the mountains,
while I look at another album filled with the showbiz headshots

and cheesy professional pictures of Aunt Linda from back when she was a go-go/nude dancer. These also show Aunt Linda with her husband, our Uncle Steve, my dad's best friend. There are promotional photos of them in their striped, bell-bottom pants and flowered, button-down shirts and groovy leather belts, back-lit with halos for hair. I see some of Uncle Steve, who was in the TCB band as well, and in some performance black-and-whites that someone took at the Pussycat-a-Go-Go, even some of Linda in a go-go girl cage. I recall that Aunt Linda used to brag that she had the first breast job in Vegas, and she was very proud of it. I remember her encouraging me to touch it, and that her chest felt hard.

Aunt Linda used to send us to the 7-11 for Kools and Gallo port wine with a note for the clerk and give us a little extra cash for penny candy, which I loved. There are a handful of pictures from a Halloween party that my parents had, when Aunt Linda came into the garage bedroom where we were sleeping, dressed like a sexy leopard, the year she did a drunken striptease for us in the middle of the night. She didn't reveal anything scandalous except some barely showing pasties, and she used her long costume leopard tail to bonk my brother, Jack, on the head. In the party photos, she looks tipsy. I remember thinking that she had the strangest job of all of them, even weirder than the friends' dads who were craps dealers.

I like the pictures of my dad's lounge acid-jazz band signing a record contract, and then backing Andy Williams, some of him on tour with Elvis, and a few of the families meeting the band at the airport as they returned from Hawaii after filming a concert. There are even a few informal poses of me and my mom in the matching Hawaiian print mumu dresses that dad brought back. In some of the photos you can tell that the lifestyle was starting to wear on my mom – she looks tired and uncomfortable. There's a page where she has us three kids, and she's surrounded by musician guys and their skimpily-attired nude dancer girlfriends. In a handful of the photos of her before kids, my mom is wide-eyed and beautiful, like a French actress filtered through the dirty south, showing her at bohemian parties in Paris and Pisa. You can see her heritage – that she came from a long line of early Americans, but ended up on the mixed-race side of her family tree.

I love the cracked and faded photos of her family, I note the generations and passed-down features of her ancestors – the French, Scotch-Irish, the Black, the Native Americans who survived The Trail of Tears. In one photo with the grandmother and the clan who had to leave North Carolina for a reservation in Oklahoma, they are shown standing in front of their share-cropper's house with their horse in the photo. The Scotch-Irish folks of hers were the ones who eventually fell for the cult of Mormonism, moving further west to mind-numbingly beautiful Utah. One of my maternal grandmother's cousins had run off to live with the Shoshone Indians and had written a book about it called *White Indian Boy*, preferring that life to the life of the Mormons.

Perhaps that explains my grandmother's openness to marriage with a blood-quantum man. There are photos of grandmother as an orphan, having lost both of her parents in the Spanish Flu pandemic, after being sent to Los Angeles as a little girl to be raised by her sister, Florence, in South Central Los Angeles.

Grandmother's sister lived in Los Angeles after she met her husband, a drummer and bartender in the jazz era. The photos show family dinners with pre-fame movie stars like John Wayne, guys my great uncle had served at the Hollywood bar he tended and played drums in. Then there are the black-and-whites of my grandmother as a teen, posing with a lovely shy smile and then, after meeting up, looking romantic with my handsome Merchant Marine grandfather in Los Angeles. Then there are photos of them moving to Utah, where they relocated temporarily when my grandmother was pregnant and my grandfather was on submarines in faraway seas in the war.

They didn't stay long in Utah after my mother was born, and quickly headed back to LA to escape small town Mormon wife- swapping. There are photos of my mom as a baby right after the Allies beat the Nazis, still in Utah, in my grandfather's arms, with his wavy dark hair and brown skin contrasting with my mom's infant white baby skin and pale white hair. There are photos of mom's childhood home after they moved back to Los Angeles, a modest cottage with my grandfather's TV repair shop in the garage, a pack of wild kids in the front, and an orange grove behind the house.

Shots fill a few pages of my mom and dad as teens growing up in the beatnik surfer era and then early rock and roll Los Angeles, from when they met in high school. My teenage dad looks like a band nerd, and my kid mom looks like a wild thing. My dad's family had a nice house on a nice street, and his parents both worked for nice local companies, trading work shifts to bring up the children.

Then my parents are standing in front of the Little Church of the West, the chapel from the movie *Viva Las Vegas*. In their wedding photos, in front of the Frontier casino on the Strip, both of them look to me like gorgeous movie stars, my mom's tiny belly with my brother inside, beginning to show. In those wedding photos, you can see the spectrum of my ancestry lined up in a row of faces, from dad's cousin Vincenzo standing next to to my maternal femme fatale, Aunt June, as the two of them were dating. Aunt June is also standing next to her mom, my sweet-faced and patient looking grandmother. In some of them my dad looks happy and my mom looks excited, hands on her belly. Dad's mother looks protective of my mom, with her arm around her pregnant waist. Dad's dad looks peeved, like he's mad that his son didn't get to be the Las Vegas playboy he'd hoped he would be.

Chapter 4
Tell Me Why

As I drift around at the old elementary schoolyard, I observe my best friend in kindergarten as she wears her hair in a bouffant on picture day, hanging upside down from the monkey bars to prove that it was real and not a wig. I remember her mom serving us peanut butter and jelly sandwiches, with her hair in a similarly fluffy updo. I behold the circus twins, called the Flying Farnellis, who would do tricks on the playground during recess for an enraptured crowd of kids.

The Farnelli family, including their parents and older siblings, worked nights and weekends at Circus Circus, and the twins with their pierced ears had to wear thread instead of earrings, because their mom worried they would get their earlobes ripped during a triple flip. I recall how so many of the kids had fathers like mine who worked in the orchestras and casinos, some parents professional gamblers, some bartenders, some cocktail waitresses. I recall their uniforms and work badges, their comings and goings in their cars to and from jobs down at the casinos.

I prowl through the classrooms, starting in my first grade room, observing myself and my buddy on the day when she invited me to go to her house for lunch, saying we could make tuna melt sandwiches. Upon arrival, her mother was so drunk all she could do was scream at us from the couch.

We didn't havesandwiches that day. I hang around, silently, in our second grade room because the teacher was mean and scary, while reminiscing about our neighbor Roy's dad, who was always passed out from drinking, and how it was easy to get money from his pants pockets for after school candy at the Stop n' Go. Most of my second grade recollection is a haze of purloining money for after school treats from passed out neighbor dads' pockets and my fear of that grumpy teacher.

I float through a partition to the third grade room and have a vision of the day I tested out of regular classes and was placed in an advanced program for the weird kids. I hover over myself in that classroom while I make a cardboard diorama back-drop for models of unseen deep sea fish that I had researched and then shaped, glazed and baked using ceramic clay. This class that allowed us to create projects about the things in which we were most interested. I was fascinated by the fish that lived in complete darkness and, at that time, there were no photographs, just etchings documented in encyclopedias. I see myself stand up in the diorama and pretend to breathe underwater with them, enfolded in the black tempera-painted background.

I skim over the fourth grade playground, the year I was recruited by the boys in the neighborhood to play basketball because I was tall and could shoot baskets from the years practicing with my first boyfriend. I brood over how I would play all year until nightfall after school and even well into the summer, because that was the year I learned how to street fight. I quickly waft past the boys' bathroom of my fifth grade year, recalling that I had gained a reputation for fighting rough when the boys would pick fights with me on dares from one another. I hover over myself as I scrap with them for bullying another kid and, as I chase them down and throw them to the ground, sitting on them and pummeling the areas of their faces that are most vulnerable. I feel ashamed of my violence.

I move over to the sixth grade yard and onto the bus as we are shuttled across town in buses to get white kids into the area where Vegas still needed integration, into the Northtown neighborhood that was a holdover from the era when the clubs and casinos were still segregated. I watch us smoke a roach on the playground with the teenaged musician guys from across the street, as they push the roach clip through the chain link fence at lunch and, afterward, how we try to run President Carter's fitness course or play soccer, stoned during PE class, with our PE teacher sometimes giving us surprise math tests if she suspected or caught the smell on our clothing.

As I loiter around our sixth grade center, there's a flash in my mind of a scene of us as we decided to become blood sisters, out on the yard. Someone had brought a pocket knife, and we sat under a tree and made nicks on our palms and rubbed them on one another's hands. The principal found us and took us to the nurse who lectured us about people who cut off their hands and sent them to the mayor in a box.

I stand for a while in my math classroom, observing the teacher as he takes the whole month of October to read us the Son of Sam serial killer book. When he finishes, he holds up a picture of the Son of Sam and says he is him. A girl in the front row screams and runs out of the classroom. He then laughs and shows the classroom the photo, and he looks exactly like Son of Sam.

I fly away from the schoolyards and into our childhood neighborhood and watch us on weekends or during summers. The summers we spent riding bikes, or sometimes horses, as far out into the desert as possible. We go to the Charleston Theater for Ray Harryhausen triple features. My mom's brother, in and out of prison for heroin possession or smuggling, lives with us sometimes between prison stays. He has a bullwhip and an old

working Winchester rifle and a rusty Chevy truck from the 1950s
with a camper shell that he made from scrap lumber on the back.

He puts out lawn chairs for thunderstorms during the flash
flood season. He gets drunk, and we watch the lightning. I see our
family lineage in his sharp features and tan skin, as we go on bike
rides with him, a six-pack hanging from his handlebars and, as he
drinks through the cans, we ride far out past the rodeo and pow-
wow arena and into the wash, then out past the trailers with the
tweakers and desert rats. I stand over him, passed-out drunk in
the dirt, and observe as my brothers and I ride back to a 7-11 to
call our parents for a way back to town.

Sometimes we get into the back of his Chevy and
ride out to the freshwater hot springs at the edge of nowhere,
encircled within an oasis of cottonwoods and its nests of
baby rattlers, its crawly little scorpions, and watch as we find
arrowheads and fossils of ancient deep sea creatures that I am
collecting for my diorama. We shoot the old rifle at rusty beer
cans, trying to focus our aim with skinny arms and not fall
with the kick. In the back of his pickup under the homemade
camper shell on those truck rides, we are always tossed around
going over the rough roads, rolling around in the back with his
tools and sleeping bags. We would go with him to explore old
mining caves and ghost towns that were not on the maps. We
would come home from these adventures with old whiskey
bottles and pickaxes, or sometimes a bull snake for a stew or to
keep as a pet.

We take our Honda 80s out for long rides, sometimes
crashing into cactus or burning our legs on the tailpipes, or we
take out the retired rodeo horse, three of us cousins on her bare
back, riding her up to the foot of Sunrise Mountain. The first year
that our grandpa got a boat, we would go out to Lake Mead a lot.
We would pile as many Italians into it as we could fit, and the
tiny little vessel would ride low over the water, filled with all of
us, and out to the island near the harbor. On the island, we would
dock and swim around the shiny oil slicks making rainbows in

the sun on the surface, us taking turns learning how to water ski. We eat chicken salad sandwiches and sit in the sun, feeding pink popcorn to giant, ugly carp.

I wish someone would tell me why I am not able to walk back into these hallucinations. I want to be with them or just go home.

Chapter 5
I Call You a Friend

I'm drifting through more visions of the summer before seventh grade, as everyone is breaking into the model homes near the school to drink Coors and make out in the staged bedrooms. My brother and his friends dig forts in the last remaining patch of land near the new houses and put plywood over them and cover them with dirt. The hatches lead to crude steps that go down underneath the dirt and cactus.

I recall being stoned down there with Jenny the summer between seventh and eighth grade. Jenny was my friend from sixth grade, and this is where my visions get foggy, maybe from the drugs she did, the ones I tried. She used to take her dad's pain pills, and we would ride the city bus around Vegas during summer break. The pills would make her sick, and she'd throw up a little bit on the floor of the bus right after taking them and then, after they kicked in, she'd be so relaxed and peaceful. Together we'd feel like we were floating inside those air-conditioned city buses. Men and boys would get on and talk to us, and we wouldn't hear them, we were so happy in our reclining psychic-sister cloud.

The little puddle of vomit would slop around a little under our feet in the traffic. From within this memory, I decided to visit Jenny. I find myself in Jenny's current bedroom, the one that's still at her mom's house, and see that she has harmed her body beyond repair. As I lay my not-hands over her abdomen, her guts feel almost completely rotten, as if her body won't tolerate any more booze, yet she keeps drinking it. She buys it by the case and keeps it in the trunk of her car and pours it in her Big Gulp cup and sips it all day and all night with diet soda. She wants to sleep but has cold sweats and constant nausea, and anxiety rips at her as soon as she lies down. It starts at her stomach and climbs up into her lungs and chokes her and won't let her rest. The chatter in her mind is so crowded with her fears, there is no room for anything else. I try to hold her close in my mind and whisper to her from this place beyond her eyesight but, when she's afraid, she has no ability to sense anything except anxiety.

I flashback to Jenny and me at thirteen when she was beautiful the way budding flowers are, flushed with immaculateness. Her dad's office is the bar next to the convenience store where we used to go get candy with stolen money. We never find him anywhere else. When she needs money for something, we go to the bar and hit him up for a few bucks. At first, that's why we are riding the bus, to go to her dad's office. We ride our bikes a few times, but then it's too hot in the summer, so we figure out how to do the transit system, and soon we go all over town that way.

We ride the bus to Circus Circus, we spend $1.99 and get the lunch buffet. It smells like a septic tank inside and has giant clowns painted on the walls. You can eat as many shrimp cocktails and prime rib as you like. Some of the regulars are there for a few hours a day, shuffling back and forth with fresh plates of mashed potatoes and salmon mousse. The jello is hard and cut in squares. I build abstract multi-colored sculptures on small plates and lay them out next to each other and stare at the light shining through.

The tiny desserts all taste like the same variety of yellow cake but have different colors of frosting, including blue and green. They play pop music, and we sing along. We kill a few hours just sitting there high and singing and making abstract art jello brick sculptures, not eating much but mostly just there for the ambience, before walking around the midway on the second floor above the gamblers, watching the showgirls ride the sky ponies and the acrobats flying over the net above blackjack tables. We meet boys on the midway and talk to them and play Skee-Ball.

Jenny always had a hole in her. She covered it up really well with her gorgeous thirteen-year-old hair and perfect white thirteen-year-old smile, but she was already finding a way to get older guys to sneak her daiquiris from the midway bar. I refused to join them. I felt the need to get us back to the east side of town. It felt like a long way home, and I needed to pay attention to get back properly. I would steer us out of there after dark and onto the Strip bus to transfer at Flamingo or Tropicana.

It appears now that Jenny is so broken her ego convinces her that no one can tell that she's been on a three-year bender. She thinks her mom can't smell it on her, that her mom is naive and lets her stay in her childhood bedroom because she's so often in between jobs or because of health problems. Her mom lets her come and go because her mom wants her to stay alive. I stand invisibly in the room watching Jenny deny that she just had a sixteen-ounce Big Gulp filled with vodka and diet Dr. Pepper for breakfast, and then see her mom stifle her tears.

I float near Jenny and, if she's not afraid, she feels like she knows I'm there, even when she's nearly passed out. She talks to me, and I talk to her. I tell her to go to a doctor, to look into going to college, to do anything but this. If she feels like I'm there, she knows I can see everything she's doing, and I know that she's deeply ashamed. Sometimes when she's talking, I'll get close to sensing what's in her heart and soothe her to sleep. Her heart is the cleanest heart I know. It's the same heart I met when we were thirteen and she was blooming.

Chapter 6
The Scene

Todd will wake up and remember me next to him at Room 13 as a band plays, before I was dark and quiet and prone to disappearance and silence sometimes. I would always come back to him until I didn't come back anymore. He still remembers me saying more than once that I was going to get the fuck out of this town someday. Then we will both recall at the same time as I lie near him together, how he professed his love for me with the ferocity of a downpour in the middle of the raging Gulf of Mexico monsoon thunderstorm of dollar beers and stage diving and all day boredom that was the reason for everything that went wrong and still always is.

In my mind, it's spring, and I'm turning fourteen. I was invited to my first Friday night keg party. My friends and I really wanted to go, so we made a flyer advertising a fake all-girl punk band called Raw Scabs, boasting that we were playing at the party. The flyer had a picture of Ronald Reagan with a safety pin piercing his nose, made out of newsprint collage, and we posted it around school so everyone would think we were actually playing, but we were still not sure we could even go because it is at was at the party mansion where the bikers dealt drugs, and my uncle, the one who cooked meth, was one of their suppliers. We still had to ask our moms for permission. The man who owned the party mansion was a brain surgeon with a serious cocaine habit. His house and his drug habit was legendary.

In the fake band, we gave ourselves tough-sounding punk rock names, so I was the bass player, Tara Ann Tula. In truth, my brother's band, Future Blues, was actually playing the party, and I had been practicing to sing a Rush song called "Tom Sawyer" with them. They practiced in the converted garage room, and the Aguapo brothers played bass and drums, and my brother, Jack, played the double-neck guitar.

Raul Aguapo had initially asked me to sing, but then he realized I wasn't the best singer, so rather than kick me out, he decided that he'd keep me but, right after practice, he'd wrestle me to the ground, and I'd have to fight my way out of the leg-trap camel-clutches and chicken-wing over-the-shoulder cross-faces and hammerlocks.

He told me he had to practice for the high school team tryouts, but he always had an erection, and I knew they were professional wrestling moves because I had been to a few professional wrestling matches at the Showboat Casino on Boulder Highway. I was always forced to harm him in a minor way to get him to unlock me. I recall myself not actually having any strong impulses to be sexual when he'd wrestle and grind on me. I had started to notice sex, as it was happening all around me, and I tried not to humiliate Raul, but I really wanted to.

I didn't want everyone to think I was uncool, but I felt the way I imagined a melting popsicle on a hot sidewalk might feel, when the ants are swarming it. It was as if I was thawing and I was losing the battle of gravity, and even if I hated the way the ants were swarming me, I was sweet to them. Everyone told everyone else what they were up to in the model homes and the backseats, and that was our sex-ed class.

It was an open secret that the surgeon who was hosting the party was one of the richest men in the neighborhood, but that he was completely insane and only partied with drug dealers because of his tremendous habit. He hired bikers to do security for him at the parties, but that was also a way for them to sell whippets from helium tanks to lines of kids for a dollar a balloon. I didn't like the bikers because they would talk to us in a creepy and stupid way, and they would look at us girls like we were piles of freshly roasted, pulled sandwich pork.

The surgeon had bought two of our modest, neighborhood tract ranch homes and made them into one large home with a pool and three stories. There was an observatory on the third floor. That's the one thing I was always curious about in that house – what the stars looked like through his telescope. I would skateboard past the house looking at the thing and thinking how much you could see in the night sky from a real observatory, wondering about seeing the rocks on the moon, or maybe left-behind-astronaut-mobile tracks, or Venus and Mars up close.

When I finally asked, my mom gave me permission to go to the party because my older brother would be there. I remember that after she said I could go, I was anxious immediately. Not only was I going to be singing that Rush song with my brother's band, but I had planned to try to sneak up to the observatory to look at the sky. At school, during the week prior to the party, we had pretended that it was going to be the debut of Raw Scabs, and we put up flyers and talked up our covers of the Sex Pistols and the Clash.

We went to great lengths to choose outfits, and I borrowed a leather mini skirt and 50s pumps and a striped top from an older friend who was good at finding the treasures at the Opportunity Village thrift shop on Decatur Avenue. I thought I looked like a French actress from an old black-and-white movie.

The morning of the show, I woke up excited like it was

Christmas, and I was petrified. A local skate punk band called
The Swell was the one we all really wanted to see, and we were
going to try to act cool, but we were nervous and scared because
we had never been to a punk gig, especially not a keg party, and
we really wanted to pass for punk rock.

We had heard that the scary punk girls who were already
in the 'scene' would try to cut our hair, and we still had long hair,
not short or shaven hair like punk chicks had. So we put our long
hair up in fake Mohawks or teased-up piles, using two cans of
Aqua Net and a package of bobby pins, and overdid our makeup
as well, trying to look like Siouxsie Sioux photos we had cut
from the National Enquirer.

We drove to the party mansion in my friend's dad's
Valiant. Even though I wasn't old enough to drive, I ended up
being the driver because I learned how to drive the year before
when my uncle was out of prison and staying with us for a few
weeks. I was already pretty good at it. He didn't have a license
from being in jail, and he thought it would be easier to have me
drive him to the store when he was drunk, to pick up smokes and
booze.

I fetched the two other fake members of our fake band
and we headed to the party, nervous and squeaky. My friends
and I arrived, and Future Blues had set up their equipment in a
big ballroom, which made me feel even more nervous because I
had never sung for a crowd except for the fifth grade talent show,
when I sang "Joy to the World-Jeremiah Was a Bullfrog" with
James Valenti whose dad had played in the TCB band with my
dad.

The large ground floor room had a disco ball and a two-
foot stage and a fireplace and a wet bar. Older guys at the bar
were serving underaged kids beer, and shitty weed was being
passed around in a ceramic wizard bong. I skipped the weed and
was handed a bottle of Michelob beer from one of the bikers
tending the bar. I saw my friends go outside to the patio, and I

followed them.

I noticed right away that there were some very cute boys leaning against a palm tree planter, and one caught my eye, and I smiled at him, and he grinned back but, just as I started walking to where my friends were, I was jumped by two tiny girls with short hair, just like the story in the B-movie script I had been worrying over in my head for the past few weeks. My first thought was that they were going to try to cut my hair. Instead, one jumped on my back and tried to take me down, while the other one began weakly striking me in the face with her spiked bracelets.

I shifted into scrappy school girl mode and saw red, like in the Saturday morning cartoons. I leaned over with one girl on my back, who was holding onto my hair like I was a horse, and I broke the bottle on the concrete and, with the bottleneck in my hand, turned my torso to throw her hard onto the ground. She kept holding onto my hair, which put my face in her face as I sat on her, suddenly holding the broken glass of the beer bottle to her neck. The one with the bracelets was hitting me on the back of the head but, as soon as she realized I was stronger and ready to maybe cut her friend, she backed off. Some of the guys who had been laughing at us during the initial attack, including the one I thought was extra cute, stopped laughing and moved both the girls away from me and looked at me with semi-impressed faces.

I stood up and felt the damage to my face and head because whatever they had done to me included some bleeding. I felt messed up and confused, and I was wondering why I was still holding the broken Michelob beer bottle in my hand. A biker who was standing and watching the whole thing, a man who had been snickering with a crowd of older guys, came up to me and asked if I was okay. I said I wasn't sure, and I asked if he could show me where the bathroom was so I could clean up.

He told me that I looked sexy with a bloody face as he took the broken bottle from my hand and held it up while the guys on the backyard patio laughed and clapped. I was not impressed with myself for fighting, I was still reeling and dizzy, with a slow trickle of liquid from my scalp running down my nose and onto my shirt, and the feelings of shame about fighting were flooding over me like I was a kid again.

The bathroom was up one flight of stairs, and it was adjacent to a bedroom with another wet bar, decorated like a divorced dad's corny sex chamber. The walls were covered with gold-tint and black-veined faux marble-print floor-to-ceiling mirrored 12" x 12" tile, even in the shower. It looked to me like a decorating disaster that would be hard to clean the Vegas hard water stains off of. I was able to get an overhead view in these mirrors of the blood that was matting my hair and starting to drip lightly from the small cuts on my head, down my face and onto the shag carpeting. I felt a little bit like Carrie after the prom, but I soaked some toilet paper and dabbed at the cuts, and I noticed that, even though they were small, they were producing a decent amount of blood.

There was a cut on my nose that seemed to have a significant drip, so I blotted it and used a washcloth to try to get it to stop. It wouldn't stop, so I held the washcloth to it while I tried to clean some of the blood out of my hair. That wasn't working either, so I just kind of mashed it back into a pile and used the drying clots to hold some of the floppier thatches in place, like a Dippity-Doo gel.

I tried to fix my makeup, but my face was smeared with dark red crust. I decided to wash my face with the Irish Spring on the basin, and I got the makeup and blood off and dried my face and head with the towel on the rack.

When I went into the hall again, the older biker guy was waiting for me with a couple of glasses filled with booze, and the drinks resembled a glowing sunset. He said, "It looks like you could use a stiff drink after all that."

I really didn't have my wits about me, and I had never heard anyone say stiff drink before, aside from the way they talked in old movies, but I took one of the glasses and downed a large gulp while he tried to flatter me by telling me what a serious brawler I was, which I found annoying and not a compliment, and then I felt ashamed again.

I took another smaller sip and started to feel dizzy and disoriented. He took me by the elbow and asked me if I had seen the house. In my hazy stupor, I said no but that I had heard about the observatory and asked him if I could see it. He said yes and steered me through rooms filled with taxidermy and animal trophies that had been made into furniture and decorations, strange erotic carvings, and other exotic things that looked like the kind of stuff rich people with bad taste collected. We finally made it up the last flight of stairs to the observatory and into some chairs that I could lean back in. The large telescope was pointing out through a domed glass ceiling window.

I woke up a few hours later face down on a child's twin bed. It was the kind with a fake oak wagon wheel headboard. I was in pain and undressed. Someone was covering me with a blanket and someone else was shaking me.

I had been gone from the party since I went to clean up after the fight and my friends had all been drinking. They had discussed looking for me when my brother's band started to play and I was supposed to sing, but then they couldn't find me so they figured I was off somewhere. Everyone went on to enjoy the bands and get drunk and, when it was time to go home, they realized they hadn't seen me since we arrived and so they started searching in earnest.

They discovered that house was even weirder than we thought, and that parts of it were blocked from access. They found a basement level which was accessible from a hidden back hallway. They finally located me behind an unlocked closet door.

When they found me, the bedroom was not disorderly, the two beds in the room were made. I was on top of one of them and, when they first saw me, they assumed I had maybe gone in there with some other drunken random person to fool around.

But when they sat me up and forced my clothes on me, they noticed the bleeding between my legs and the bruises on my neck. They looked at one another and decided to ignore it.

My friends carried me to the car, drove me back to one of their houses and then put me on a hard and uncomfortable sofa bed for the night with a blanket and pillow. My scalp still hurt and bled a little, but my body and mind were numb.

I went to bed and slept through the pain, and I woke up in the morning on a bloodstained blanket that I folded and wrapped around me like a cape, and I walked home in the borrowed thrift store pumps.

Chapter 7
There Is No Love

I'm curled up next to Todd as he rests on his bed. He's got the TV on the news with the volume low, as he's thinking about the party back in the day where he watched Janis and Maxine attack me. He's thinking about how I had walked out on the back deck at that surgeon's place with a beer and caught his eye and smiled, and how I had looked so out of place. He's in his bed at his home behind the enormous Vegas World tower, and he was startled when he first woke up because he has been sleeping away from there for a few months. His estranged wife and son have moved out of this house, and he's been considering the reality that his son will have a new stepfather soon and how much newer that home is compared to this one.

He reminisces about how I walked out on the deck at the party where they were playing later that night, where the bikers were giving everyone in his crowd lines of speed, and how he and Mike both looked at me at the same time and started bragging to each other about who would grab me as I smiled right at them. *Grab* was code for *take to the abandoned house.* As soon as they started talking about me, they saw me get jumped by the other girls. He chuckles to himself remembering how fast it was over, how roughly I tossed the smaller one off my back and pinned her with a beer bottle that I broke right before she hit the ground. He remembers laughing at us but getting tense when Maxine started hitting the back of my head with her bracelets after I sat on Janis, remembers that Maxine figured out how tough I was and stopped herself before he had to stop her. None of them had ever seen me before that night. He remembers that I disappeared right after, figuring that I had probably been too afraid and humiliated to stay at the party.

He recalls that the next time he saw me was in a garage at that hesher kid's house in my neighborhood about six months later, where The Swell was playing on the east side. That I looked different, older, and that I stood motionless by the side of the mosh pit, watching, unfazed, unsmiling. He pictures how he sang and tried to catch my eye so he could smile at me like he had done at the party, but how I just stared at the hands of the musicians, studying intensely, like I was trying to decrypt some kind of code that only boys with guitars knew.

There was an abundance of beer at the east side party, as someone had gone on a run and come back with at least ten cases of Coors, but he recalls how I wasn't drinking like the rest of the kids. How I was dressed in jeans, my brother's old army boots, and a white t-shirt with a band name drawn on with a sharpie and, while the other girls had on makeup that was an attempt to create the effect of being British in 1977, he noted that I wasn't even wearing lipstick. That he liked how I looked, because my hair was still long and not put up in a fake Mohawk or whatever, like the first time he had seen me.

He noted with a smile that he, too, had mostly worn jeans and t-shirts and his leather motorcycle jacket back then, and had been telling the guys at practice earlier in the week before the garage show that he was tired of trying to get through layers of fishnet and crinoline and bustiers and bondage buckles and eyeliner and lipstick and hairstyles just to have a good time with whatever girl he was able to grab.

He sees in this memory of the east side party how I had gone outside after the band had played and sat by the pool in a lounge chair. The house was a two story, and he could tell the family was comfortable by how they had furnished it. The parents were out of town, so the kids had the run of it for the night. There was a deck above the pool by the master bedroom, where they were congregating, and some of the boys were jumping off the balcony into the pool wearing their leather jackets and jeans.

He likes remembering how I was getting splashed and that it was funny to see the eyeliner smearing on the faces of the boys, as their liberty spikes drooped over their white pancake makeup. He starts thinking about the punk boys and how some of them acted like bower-birds, each one attempting a more fantastic hairdo and those many layers of garments and ornamentation as a mating call to the girls who were dressing like broken dolls and hyperactive whores. He loves remembering how the whole thing was such a middle finger to the 1980s and his Mormon dad who always dressed in beige, with his stocks and cubicle and Crown Victoria, the dad who wanted him to listen to AM Christian country music and play sports and who told him frequently that he found him to be a terrible disappointment.

He laughs remembering how he watched me as I started laughing because a few kids started shaking up cans of beer and splashing the bystanders and how they splashed me and the kids in the pool. Todd remembers mustering up his courage to go talk to me as I smiled from getting sprayed with beer out by the pool, how he decided to make an attempt before I could disappear again. He recalls how he grabbed two cans of beer and came over and asked me if he could "get in on the beer fountain action," how I nodded yes, how I smiled at him the way I did at the keg party before I disappeared, and how I made room for him on the lounger by bending my knees and scooting up my feet.

I am in my own memories now, lying next to him, and I remember how he sat on the edge of the chair and asked if I wanted one of his beers. How I said yes, and he cracked it, and I took a gulp. How I told him I liked the watery taste, and that it was the same beer that my dad had let me sip when I was little. He took a long draw and burped, and called it "delicious Rocky Mountain beaver piss." I remember that I smiled at him and noticed the thing that I instantly liked about his face as he grinned after making what he thought was an incredibly droll remark, was that he looked both battle-worn and innocent, like a cartoon bear that had been through a few forest fires but made it out of all of them alive, but still a little singed.

I think of our conversation, how Todd had asked me my name and how old I was. He told me that he was sixteen and he was the youngest guy in his band, The Swell. I remembered that I didn't look him in the face the whole time they had played at the east side party and didn't realize he was the singer that time when they were playing, because I was so focused on what the musicians were doing to their guitars with their hands. He told me he went to Rancho High and lived on the west side, asked me if I'd been to the skate park on that side of town. He told me his family was Mormon and that his mom had breast cancer. He told me that he wanted to talk to me at the keg party and that he had seen me get beat up, and asked if that's why I had left early and didn't come and talk to him. He told me he thought my hair was pretty, and then how come I was being "so quiet." I had shrugged and told him that I wanted to play bass and, that before he came to sit next to me, I was thinking about it. I told him that I needed a bass and asked if he knew where I could get one. He said that he had a spare one I could borrow, and he asked me if he could give me his phone number and if he could have mine. I remember how I stopped to think about it for a minute as I got nervous, and how he looked into my eyes and stared laughing and chiming out, "You're a goofy chick, I like you."

Slipping out of these memories, I look at Todd's peaceful face lying there running through these thoughts, and I think this

way of remembering together is my tether to his love, and I want
to be with him, I want to be alive and warm to the touch. He
thinks he feels me next to him and, even though he thinks he's
imagining it and that that makes him crazy, he still feels good
and right about it in his gut. He gets up and gets ready for work,
so I float along with him in his car and into the casino restaurant
where he's the head chef working swing shift, and I watch him
make the line cooks worry after he goes into the bathroom for a
few long minutes.

When he comes out of the bathroom, he's talking fast
and not being nice, and I realize that he is now coked-out. I feel
angry with him, and I decide to push some glasses from the shelf
I'm standing next to in the kitchen as he quickly brushes past
me, because he's much too high. Two side-by-side pint glasses
fall and break on the floor, and he bends down to clean them up,
cursing everyone including me out loud, even though he's not
consciously aware I'm there, still next to him, fucking with him
invisibly but on purpose.

He cuts both his hands picking up the broken glass,
because he can't feel the pain very well when he's that high,
and then the blood flows out. I crouch next to him and reach
and hold his hands in not-mine. He sits on the floor and starts to
silently sob thinking I'm there, holding his bleeding hands out
and looking like a madman. The line cooks try not to laugh at
him because he looks so insane, so as to avoid getting fired, and
now he is angry with them and cursing at them, too.

As he sits on the floor of the kitchen bleeding onto the
floor, he goes back in his mind to the day I disappeared, and to
the feeling of how he woke up badly hungover with a Rummel
Motel matchbook on the toilet tank that he was certain wasn't
there the night before. Right after I died, I had also put the copy
of the *Fear and Loathing* paperback we were taking turns reading on the floor of his van. The Rummel was the cheap place on
the Strip at Sahara where he spent the last week of my life.

We started staying there together in the summer, and the entrancing machine hum of the air conditioning kept the street noise out of the room. We slept all day, listened to music at night, ate very little except for leftovers he brought from his work, and read and played our guitars, or talked and fooled around the rest of the time. He had a small amount of money from a job he did three nights a week, because he had been promoted to waiting tables at the Peppermill on the Strip, which paid for the room throughout the fall and winter.

When I died, school was out for winter break, and all during the prior fall I didn't want anyone to know I was staying with him at the motel off and on because of my age, and so he had to act like he was just my friend at the Room 13 shows. That would make him feel like saying catty things to me and heckle me when the band I had started playing bass in began playing shows, which I liked because he was hilarious and it was attention from him. He always assumed my desire for secrecy was because I wanted to be with the other guys behind his back, but what the truth was, I wasn't able to tell him then.

After death, I could finally know the hunger of his equal weakness for me, and how deathly afraid I was of his power over me. The memory of the feelings and the sweetness of all the things I would never say and how those were the best nights of my life would have killed me again, if I was still alive. But I was there, dead, holding his hands in the restaurant, with my mind soaring out to the warm nights when we laid down on the sleeping bag on the side of the road next to the van, because I told him I wanted to look at the stars, remembering the feeling of his soft hair in my hands and how the canopy of stars behind his head contrasted with the rough ground under the thin sleeping bag beneath us. I wanted to feel the nothing and every-thing that was my life all at once when I was next to him on the rocky ground. I wanted to feel the blood coursing under the thin flesh of his neck and the skin above it pulsing against my lips. And memories of being alive underneath him are still excruciating.

The hostess walked into the kitchen, after a line cook had gone to tell the her that something bad was going on, and she gave Todd a sharp and nervous look. He was a talented chef and still good- looking in a slightly wasted sort of way, and they would sleep together sometimes when he could make it happen, so she didn't want him to get fired. She tapped his arm. He noticed that blood was dripping on his pants and the floor and how he was crouching there like an idiot, so he stopped crying and barked out a command that sounded like a coyote howl, for her to *get him a wetfuckingtowel!*

She wet a few of the dry cotton dishcloths at the sink and brought them to him, and he mopped up the blood first and then wrapped his hands, then stood up and put a bunch of the takeout rubber bands over the towels, and went back to the line. He glared at the cooks who were containing their laughter as I watched the pulse leak out and seep into the rough white cloth.

Chapter 8
Life As War

I have a terrible vision that I am alive, and it's the time after the party mansion night, and I want to wake up from it. I cannot piece back together what must have been roughly six hours of my life, and I feel the pain and bleeding between my legs that lasts too long afterward and how I could not tell anyone. How I just wore pads and felt intense pain like I was being punched and kicked in the stomach, and how it made it hard to walk normally for a while.

The back of my neck had dark bruises where a man's large hands had been, and my mind had been full of murkiness and deadness, like a gray fog I could not escape. The back of my head hurt for a while after that night, too, and it felt bruised on the inside. I hated remembering how I would fall asleep in my bed at home but wake up in a cold sweat for no reason on the floor.

When I would wake up at night, I could hear my muffled shouting, feel myself fighting for breath like I was being strangled, and the sound of a stranger's voice saying *that*

no one loves me and no one will ever come to help me and how I
will die there that way.

I remember how I would lie there on the floor in a fetal
position, listening to loud but muddy distant songs playing in
my mind on a loop, and feel nothing but apprehension until
the songs ended. Then my mind would go dark, and I could
abruptly sleep again. I would wake up on time for school in the
morning, check the bruises and pain and cuts and put makeup
over them, how I would notice them as they started to fade,
and how I would stare into the mirror at the face of a stranger,
someone looking past me.

My parents had given me a separate phone line in my
bedroom for my birthday that I used to talk to my friends, and
it had started ringing all the time, late at night. The caller would
disguise his voice to sound like a younger person with a feminine
lilt and proceed to tell me what I had worn that day while calling
me "baby," and then attempt to tell me how much he liked what
we had done together at the party and how much he wanted to
do it again, and about how he wanted to kill me, trying to get to
details in his description before I hung up on him. He had started
to call every night. Part of me desperately wanted to know what
had happened, but I couldn't breathe when I heard the sound of
his voice, so I began to unplug my phone at 8 pm, and I told my
friends that my parents had given me a phone curfew and not to
call.

I recall how my friends had noticed that I was becoming
quiet and had withdrawn from hanging out with them, and that I
was dressing differently and wouldn't talk to them much, if
at all. They decided to force me to go with them to the county
fair, a Vegas tradition called Helldorado Days, held every May
around the end of the school year. A group of my friends,
including Jenny, took me to the rodeo and then to the carnival
afterward, thinking that if we had a wild night and maybe met
some boys, that maybe they could move me out of the dead
limbo I seemed to have sunk into and back into living in the

moment with them like things had been before. I remember how we drank some cheap sweet, chilled Andre pink champagne in the parking lot after the rodeo, and then they went into the carnival hollering and laughing, me quietly trailing behind them. My celebration with them was hollow, but the companionship was appreciated.

I like thinking of how we walked around the carnival eating cotton candy, allowed some of the boys who flirted with us to talk to us, and took turns going on rides with each other. The rides had made my friends woozy, but they had helped my mind shift gears, the motion had worked like the car rides did in my childhood by lulling me into peaceful meditation. The rides that flung me around upside down were the best that night, so I went on the Zipper ride with each of my three friends, but they would only go with me once each. I laugh thinking of how I went back for more, standing in line to be paired with whomever was also riding solo. I recall that I went on a few with kids my age, once with a middle-aged woman who didn't enjoy it and screamed the whole time, another time with a young dad who laughed loudly while his kids waited below.

My mind went cold as I suddenly remember the guy who got on the ride and didn't say hello. How as the ride jerked to a start and as soon as we were spinning in that harsh, circular, vertical motion, as the cage whirred upside down and right side up, the high lilt and badly-disguised voice from the phone came out of nowhere. "Hi baby, I knew I'd be with you again someday." I felt again the terror that had moved straight into my heartbeat as adrenaline flooded my nervous system and shut down my body and made the inside of my skull ache.

My hands began to tremble as I was holding onto the interior bars that the carnies pull over you. It was impossible to manage the rotation of the cage without holding on, but I was already flopping like a rag doll as one of his hands was abruptly touching my face and trying to part my legs. When he went to pull my legs apart, he couldn't because they were blocked by the safety bar and belt. I tried to fight him, causing me to lose hold of the bars, and suddenly my head and neck were flailing with the movement of the ride. He kept talking to me in that high lilt that I had heard on the phone – even as I screamed – telling me what he had done. I couldn't see him as we spun through the darkness, and I shrieked to shut out his violent words. My hair was flying in my face, covering my eyes. Then quickly the ride jerked to a stop, and the carny threw open the cage door and swiftly popped up the bars, and the man with the disguised voice turned to get off the ride. I saw a leather vest with a large patch on the back, a rustle of long stringy hair, and then he was gone.

Chapter 9
Notes from the Underground

When I was alive, as the spring turned to summer, and the valley was exceptionally oven hot and thick with smog, on some days the bowl of heat made thermometers register at 127 degrees Fahrenheit. I slept all day and stayed up all night, with tinfoil on the windows and just a bed sheet for covers. An older guy in the punk scene had rented a warehouse in the industrial part of town with the money he got from selling weed, and he was putting on shows a few nights a week, his start-up costs covered by his drug sales. He was charging two to three dollars to see four bands at least two nights a week, and he called it Room 13. Suddenly there was a tour circuit for hardcore and underground bands, and Las Vegas became a destination for a national network of DIY musicians from across the country who wanted to play there because of the reputation of moral decay and the overall sordid strangeness of Las Vegas.

I went to the gigs with my older brother who had a truck, and my life started to revolve around sleeping after school in order to stay out all night listening to the music and going to after-parties on the weekends in apartments, suburban tract homes, or hotel/motel rooms all over the hot summer Strip. I found this deeply preferable to the druggy carnivals, redneck rodeos and hard rock arena shows I had been going to with my friends before the assault, because all of that reminded me of the man who stalked me at the carnival and would still call me all the time. I was terrified of him in a raw animal way, of him finding me again, but I was determined to leave all of that behind, and the aggression and anger of the music was helping.

The music was fast and had the violence and urgency that I found comforting. We danced in spaces that we called pits, in swirling circles filled with dancers we called moshers. The boys would dive from the six-foot stages we built out of stolen lumber and nails, into one another on the floor of the pit. They would throw their arms and fists and whirl in frenzy and crash into each other with violent affection. The boys took up instruments and started playing their own versions of the three-chord anthems that we would hear on the records that we all bought at the new/ used store, the Record Exchange, that carried punk from London, New York, and Los Angeles, all of us singing in unison from the crowds or stages. The familiarity of the violence was part of the electric attraction.

I had made a new best friend, a girl named Stella, so charming and beautiful that it was impossible not to be drawn into her crazy fun whirlwind. After I met Stella, the two girls who had attacked me became my allies instead of my enemies, deciding that to fear me was to love me. Besides, Stella had a car, and soon we were all driving out on Fridays to Los Angeles to see bands at the clubs like the Cathay De Grande or places like the Olympic Auditorium. In Los Angeles, we would stay with people we had met from the tour circuit, and sometimes we would sleep in the car after the sets before driving back to Las Vegas to be back at school on Monday.

We all had skateboards, the preferred method of transpor-tation for poor kids, and we would ride them across town in the evenings to skate in abandoned and empty pools, paved drainage ditches like Jake's ditch or, if we had spending money, the skate park where The Swell would sometimes play. The Swell had changed their name to Self Abuse and went from being a fast surf-inspired band to sounding more hardcore, with nihilistic lyrics about getting wasted and hating the government. Todd became the singer of Self Abuse too, and the one time I had enough money to go to the skate park, I was able to see them perform.

I hadn't seen him since the beer fountain party where I had asked him about a bass guitar, when he told me that he would loan me his. He came up to me before they played and asked me for my phone number again, telling me he wanted to loan me the bass. He was in a hurry because they were about to play, but he handed me a pen and paper, and I wrote my number down for him. I also met Mike for the first time that day after they played. Mike was the guitar player in Self Abuse and smiled at me from the stage, and I smiled back, careful to also smile at Todd. Mike was a little older than Todd and compelling and sexy in a way that I wasn't yet familiar with. While Todd was soft and sweet, Mike seemed already dark and corrupt. Mike watched me studying him while he played his guitar during their set, and afterward came over to talk to me.

Mike introduced himself to me and then said he had overheard Todd saying he was going to loan me his bass and then aggressively offered to teach me how to play it. I was naively impressed with Mike's confidence. He had a swagger that appeared to make Todd edgy but made me feel breathless. I tried to flirt and, when Todd walked over, I said to both of them that I would take both the bass and the lessons.

My brother was leaving the skate park, so I had to leave with him and, a few minutes after I got home, the phone rang, and it was Todd. My former friends had stopped calling me that summer because I would never pick up. The phone would still ring after eight if I left it plugged in, but I never answered it. That night I did. We nervously laughed back and forth for a few minutes before we could actually have a real conversation. Then we proceeded to talk about what kind of music we liked, which bands we liked, and which bands we wanted to see live. He had a lot of records, and I didn't have as many, so he said he would be happy to educate me on the music I was missing out on.

We already had a lot in common, because we were both obsessed with music. He asked if I was going to see the new Vegas band, Subterfuge, on Friday at Room 13, and I said yes, I was planning to. We made a plan for him to give me the loaner bass there and to hang out.

Then Friday came, and it was a hot Vegas night. I had been buying 1940s and 50s dresses and vintage rodeo cowgirl boots at the Goodwill store on Charleston Street, and I was trying to dress the way the singer of my favorite band from LA looked in photos from the punk fanzines I was getting through the mail. She and her husband were writing strange poetry and singing together about bad girls and lost boys, and we were all bewitched by them. I put on my best thrift store getup, even put on makeup, and went with my brother to the warehouse. When I got there, everyone was in the parking lot, where there had just been a drunken fight. Two guys were arguing over a girl, and when the girl put her arm around one of the guys, that guy called the other guy a pussy. The pussy guy attacked the other guy, and apparently the pussy was the tougher one.

The aftermath crowd from the fight was milling around laughing about it when my brother and I got out of the truck. My brother went to find out who got beat up, while I tried to discreetly scan for Todd and Mike. I saw Todd standing in the crowd, already looking slightly drunk. He came over and took me by the hand, asking me to come to his van to get the bass. When I got to his van, he pushed me up against it and kissed me deeply as he leaned his body against mine. He was taller than me, and I was immediately melting into him, and we stood like that for as long as we could.

Mike and two of Todd's other friends saw us making out and walked over to the van and started banging on it with their fists, disrupting our moment and my first passionate kiss. One of them had a British accent and called me a *bird*, saying, "Hey Barney, who's the new bird?" Barney was apparently Todd's nickname. The other new man was blonde and looked a bit like a glam rocker. I was then introduced to Marky and Gigli, who were about to play and wanted us to come inside Room 13 and watch, adamant that we not miss any of the songs in their set.

Todd took my hand and hurried me into the warehouse because we had already missed the three opening bands, and Subterfuge was the first group from Las Vegas that everyone said sounded like a British punk band. Marky the singer was from the UK and had an accent. He was studying at the University of Nevada Las Vegas. Todd told me he knew more about original punk music than anyone else we knew.

Subterfuge started to play, and I was instantly absorbed. The pit broke out into a violent thrash, so Todd boosted me and Stella up onto the stage to keep us safe from flying elbows and army boots. Marky sarcastically mocked President Ronald Reagan in the sing-along choruses of melodic, fast and tight songs in a style that I immediately fell for. Gigli had studied his guitar riffs from the British punk bands but also the Stooges and the New York Dolls. This was the beginning of something, I thought. Far from the stoner rock bands that had continued to haunt me from the FM radio through the summer, suddenly I was pulled into a world where the music sounded the way I felt.

Chapter 10
Lost Boys

I stand next to Todd as he lies in his bed. He's living permanently in his old home again by the Vegas World tower, his wife having moved into a new home with her new partner. He's aware of me, and he's awake. He's thinking that he shouldn't have started fucking that hostess at work. He's thinking that he probably should start going to meetings again, ever since those pint glasses flew off the shelf and he had imagined that I was there holding his hands, after he bent to clean up and cut himself. He's certain that if he keeps acting like a mental patient, the hostess will stop fucking him.

He's remembering our first kiss by the car. He's remembering me smiling at him from the stage while Subterfuge played, with my red lipstick smeared on his lips. He's remembering how I wouldn't go all the way with him that night, that I shut down a little at the after- party, pulled away from him when he went to touch me under my clothing after we went to be alone in a bedroom, and how I went to look for my brother, maybe even looking at him like I would cry, he thought. He never knew why I looked at him that way.

I stand beside him, very there/not there, and I hear him breathing. I had always loved the sound of his breathing because it meant he was still alive, especially after he started using needle drugs to be more like the men in the bands he worshiped from New York and Los Angeles, shortly after he had professed to me that he had fallen in love. His body is warm, so much not like me. His body is still alive in spite of all the drugs and drinking, it is still full with circulation and blood and isn't dust and dirt and fingernails and crazy hair like mine. The warmth of his body had always been calming to me, even if it was 110 degrees out. I still craved the skin under the leather jacket and the t-shirt, deeply inside my buried bones.

My body is so dry and deeply buried, so far away from his body. There is no breathing there. His body is inside this cool house on the west side. His body is underneath a sheet and boxer shorts. My body is underneath heavy dirt and silt that will crack on the surface after the rains. I have taken to going to his home every night while he sleeps, to listen and watch. He never brings women home. He rarely watches television. He plays the guitar, he cooks and eats there, but he never does anything else besides live and sleep there. I watch him and try to send my thoughts to him. *I'm here. I love you. I should have told you what happened before we met. I'm sorry. Please stop drinking. You can't come here yet.*

Chapter 11
After the Fact

Constantly slipping back into reverie, memory, hallucination and, in my mind, I'm alive again, and it's August now, and the monsoons are coming in regularly and stronger than in past years. The downpours, lightning storms, the furious skies that soak and flood for weeks leave the desert to flower in late summer and early fall, with the smell of creosote and yucca blossoms. The shows at Room 13 are my steady habit, and I make it out to each and every show no matter what. Todd and I are together more and more even when there are no shows. He and I find it hard to be separated. Something is trying to separate us, however.

Mike had started calling me, and I would answer the phone for him, too. Our conversations were not about music, except that he would promise to give me guitar lessons and would talk in a low sexy patter while the storms pounded outside my window. He mostly talked about him, how he was going to move to Los Angeles and become famous and about us, how he felt connected to me like he had never felt before, how he could talk to me about things he couldn't talk to other women about. He said things like, "I can fuck them, but l can't talk to them."

He would tell me how exceptional he thought I was, flattering me constantly and relentlessly. He flirted with me in overtly sexual ways, in ways Todd didn't. Mike made pass after pass at me at the shows, yet I always left to make out with Todd in the front seat of his van, me on his lap, not yet his lover. Todd would show me runs on the bass and things like how to tune it, and I was learning. On another monsoon-soaked night, Todd had to work late at the Peppermill. He couldn't make it to the show that night, but Mike was there. It was just local bands, ones I had seen countless times. I spent the night not listening to the music from the stage as I usually did but in the parking lot, talking to Mike. He was telling me about notes and scales, about how to play riffs on guitar, and I was listening intently. My brother came out of the warehouse and abruptly waved me off, asking Mike if he could take me home. Mike said yes, and my brother drove off with an older girl, who looked like she knew some things. Mike was pleased, I could tell.

He had a 60s-era Mustang, the kind of car a guy from Vegas drove if he was getting it on the regular. He opened the door for me, and we got in the front seat of his car, and he turned the engine and the cassette player on. It was the sound of The Jam playing through good speakers, and I hadn't heard them before, and it was softer than what I normally listened to. It was kind of romantic and relaxing, and I suspected that was deliberate. He had a flask of fancy brandy under his seat, and he opened it, sipped it and passed it to me. I wanted to pretend like that was what I did all the time, but I had never tasted brandy before. I didn't like it, but I immediately felt flush from it, and leaned back into the seat, listened to his music and traded sips with him as he drove toward the south side. He didn't drive toward the east side where I lived, but toward where he lived. We stopped in front of a house. He reached down between his legs and eased the seat back.

As we sipped the brandy, I felt myself getting drunk, something I rarely let myself do. He started telling me that I was beautiful and that he was in love with me. He invited me to go inside the house with him, and I let him lead me to the back door where he said he had an easy way to break in. This was the abandoned house I had heard about. I did not resist. When he took me into the front room and asked me to lay down with him on the floor, I did not resist. When he pushed my skirt up and moved into me, I did not resist. When he kissed me and told me over and over that he loved me, I did not resist.

When we heard someone else open the back door, he didn't stop moving, he kept going, and whispered into my ear that I was beautiful and that he loved me and to not worry, that it was someone else who knew about the spot, that this is what they did after gigs when they didn't have a better place. When the door opened, and Todd walked into the room alone and stood watching, Mike still didn't stop moving.

I laid there stiffly and looked at Todd's face in the dark, watching his face move from surprise to accusation to hurt and anger and gloom. Mike didn't look up, he just kept moving. When Todd grabbed him by the collar of his leather jacket that he was still wearing, Mike turned his head to look at Todd and loudly yelled at him to "fucking leave!" and to leave us alone. Even after Todd backed off and left the house, and after I heard the sound of Todd's van driving away, Mike kept moving. Mike moved until he was finished, telling me over and over, "I love you, I love you, I love you." When he was done, he lay on top of me with his face in my hair. Then he drove me home and kissed me for a long time in the car before I got out.

The next day I got a call from Stella. She had heard gossip that Todd and Mike had been in a fight in front of Mike's house late the night before. Todd had driven over and waited in the van, surprising Mike as he arrived home from going out after the gig. Apparently Mike had been telling Todd from the start that he was going to do this, that he was going to grab me one night, that he would do whatever it took to get me to go to the abandoned house, like it was a contest. Todd had decided that when I didn't pick up the phone after the gig and he did our secret ring (hang up twice/call back), something was wrong. He immediately thought of the abandoned house and Mike and drove over. He told our friends that he saw Mike fucking me on the floor and that, when he walked in, Mike didn't stop, kept going, flaunted it. I asked what was being said about me, remembering my body not moving, from the floor – watching it all happen like I was frozen – and Stella said, "To be honest, Mick, *it didn't sound like it was about you at all.*"

I called Todd, who wouldn't answer. I called Mike, who did answer. He bragged that they had fought, that they were a fair match, and both of them got hurt but not seriously. I told him that I found out that he had made it clear to Todd before he grabbed me that he was going to get me to go with him. I asked him why he would try to hurt his friend that way. He snapped back, asking me why I would try to hurt his friend that way. Then he announced that he was moving to Los Angeles at the end of the summer, quitting Self Abuse to start a band called MIA and that he loved me.

I hung up and started crying, storms of tears that I had not been able to feel since before the night at the party mansion. I cried for hours, lying on my bed in a darkened room. I felt the pain from the blackout hours at the party, I felt the movement from Mike the night before. I felt guilty and like I was being abandoned, and I wished to a god that I didn't believe in that I would immediately die. I had wanted to hear those words, "I love you," so badly that I had no will of my own.

Late that night, after I passed out exhausted from sobbing, Todd finally called. He did his secret ring because it was well past 8 pm, and I picked up. He was crying, and I started crying, too, while another monsoon raged outside my tinfoil-covered window. He said he forgave me before I could speak. He said that Mike had been planning this, that he had already sworn that he would try it even though they had argued about it, and that he had been asking him not to, warning him away from me. He admitted that he was angry and hurt and told me I was an idiot to fall for his lines.

I agreed, and told him that I already knew that I had been so stupid. He said that he was angry but that he still loved me and asked if I would still see him that night. It was late, and it was raining, but I snuck out. When he arrived, I was standing on the sidewalk, soaked to the bone, and I got in his van. We drove out into the desert, and the flooding on the desolate two-lane highway stalled out the van. Todd put it in park, turned the key, set the emergency brake and climbed back onto the bench seat and pulled me from the front seat to him. I let him take the wet clothes off of me, let him put his warm dry skin on my cold wet skin. The warmth of him, the soft and then fast breathing in my ear, and then a feeling of something larger than me took over, a feeling that was both uneasy and bonding, as the pleasure from the real love I felt undid me.

He drove me home and, as we said goodbye, we both were crying. We hadn't talked much in the van. He was different, angry, I could feel it. I tried to say something, but he drove away with a strange look on his face. After that, we were closer and further apart than before. Mike was relentless and tried to see me whenever Todd was at work. I was weak, and I gave in constantly because I knew he was leaving, and his attraction to me and the words he said to me were addictive.

When Mike and I were together after the first night, he still told me he loved me over and over like a chant, and I was hypnotized by it. He taught me how to play barre guitar chords on his Les Paul and gave me a can of mace the week before he left for Los Angeles. Mike and Todd remained friends and band-mates until Mike left, but it was a hostile and unhappy tension between them that wasn't there before. I also learned, much later, that before he left for LA, he had shown Todd how to shoot cocaine and heroin, separately and then both drugs together.

Chapter 12
World of Fear

I go back to haunt the strip club where Jenny works, but she isn't there. I watch some of the dancers, who look weak and have needle marks on their bodies as they try to pretend sensuality, and I start to feel desolate. I go to Jenny's mom's house, and I don't find her there. I drag all the motels she stays at on Fremont Street and finally find her with a new man, someone who looks strangely familiar. They are smoking from a small square of tin foil using a glass straw. I stand there, furious with her, raging in spectral silence. *HOW COULD YOU, WE PROMISED*, I scream.

The vice that had captivated Mike and then Todd had invaded Las Vegas like a plague the fall of the year I died. What had once been difficult to get had become easy to get and easy to get addicted to. Meth labs were all over town, and the trio of amphetamine, cocaine, and heroin was becoming fashionable in the punk scene, many kids emulating the newer bands they liked and were trying to copy, what was happening in fabled, legendary, punk rock Los Angeles.

Jenny and I had told each other in sophomore year at school that maybe we would try it but promised to never ever

EVER EVER get addicted. My intense desire to scream at her from beyond life was frustrated by my lack of being alive, but I did send her my rage from beyond and was astounded to realize she could feel me. She looked up a few times to the spot where I was floating, but kept smoking and then falling into a blissful, itchy repose.

It had been difficult for me to use drugs like my friends had been using when I was alive. I was concerned about everything, I had grown up watching addicts suffer and withdraw, lie/steal/cheat to get high, and survival meant being aware of my surroundings at all times, trying to never let my vigilance down or let myself be caught off guard. Todd was with me at the end, but he was gone even while he was there and still angry with me and hurt by me. I knew that Mike had used cocaine off and on when he lived in Las Vegas, but I never realized the extent to which he was using until after I died and I could visit him when I was uninvited and see the extent.

Bikers had started to run the drug scene, and the punks were mixing more and more with them. I was wary of them and angry-looking whenever they were around, which was all the time by then. After getting harassed a couple of times by them at gigs, I decided to start my own band, thinking that if they weren't afraid of my friends, maybe I could make them afraid of me. I had learned enough bass and guitar by then to mangle a set list of songs properly. I found three other people, all guys, to write songs with, and we named the band Buried Alive.

The songs were angry and fierce, and we were strange and not as polished as the other bands, but people liked us and wanted us to play. We opened for a number of the more popular touring bands during that school year, and I was juggling my music and my homework at night regularly. Todd was supportive and proud of me for playing music, but he would not let me drop out of school when I whined about wanting to just play music and go on tour. He was also mildly competitive with me about our bands and coldly silent if my shittier band got more attention than his better band did. He would heckle me from the floor, calling me names. We both knew he was only half-kidding, and it made me laugh and wince.

The year I died he was in his senior year of high school but, because of his drug use, he was barely showing up for school. His dad, a conservative Mormon, eventually kicked him out because his mother had cancer, and it was all too much for them. In the winter of that year, he started staying with friends, including girls we both knew. I was ironically glad I had always insisted on condoms with both him and Mike, as if that alone would keep me from harm or death. When Todd was promoted from busboy to server at work, he started staying in shabby motel rooms near the restaurant. He would call me and ask me to come and stay with him after his shifts. Sometimes I would, telling my parents I was staying with friends.

Through the fall and early winter, he chose to stay at the Rummel Motel, which was close enough to his work to walk, but not too close, and it became his home. The season was strange, as I watched my friends go off the deep end with drugs and alcohol, and I remained sober. Christmas was particularly depressing that year. The air was bleak, and the town felt lonely and void. The one thing that cheered me up was the Social Distortion show at the casino, Vegas World, right across from the Rummel Motel. Social D was a scrappy new punk band from LA. The only problem was, they were also expert junkies, and all the boys wanted to be them, and all the girls wanted to be with them.

They loved to hang out and party after the gigs they played, and they always brought the top shelf drugs from Los Angeles with them. Social Distortion played on one of the nights after Christmas but before New Year's Eve that winter, the quiet time we called the taint of the holidays. The night of the show was a happy night for Todd. Subterfuge and Self Abuse opened the show, and everyone in the bands and most of the crowd was inebriated, to the point where there was almost a riot. Todd got so

high, he forgot that his mom was dying, that I had been fucking
Mike, and that he had stopped going to school. He had so much
fun, he bled.

Everyone was in high spirits and full of holiday cheer
while the bands were playing. I was also having fun, I had even
had a couple of beers in the parking lot with my friends, just
enough to make me want to dance in public.

The bikers were making the rounds in the parking lot
selling drugs before the show. One of the drug dealers that night
was my uncle. He was selling meth that he cooked to my punk
friends now. Having become one of the biggest meth cooks in
town, he was always looking for people who could sell for him
and would troll rock shows and now punk shows for kids he
could wrangle into an internship of sorts. He had a couple of
younger guys from my school selling for him there, and now he
was looking for people to sell for him at social events.

The crowd my uncle ran with was made up mostly of the
bikers from the surgeon's house, who sold drugs but also worked
as security for non-gang affiliated drug suppliers, escorting them
to events so that they could deal to anyone in the parking lots
and not worry about cops showing up. The bikers and the police
in Vegas had an agreement, so it was a savvy business decision
to bring at least two of them when you went to work the lots
and scout for new recruits. The two he brought that night were
sketchy and dried out, and one was familiar-looking to me and
gave me a morbid and dreary sense of deja vu.

Todd was making better money as a server at the
Peppermill now, so he had purchased a significant amount of
a few kinds of drugs from the bikers before the bands played,
enough to get the entire after party high, in addition to the
LA drugs Social D had brought along. What had been a near
riot at the club became an actual riot at the house we called
Apartment 66. Furniture was jumped on, food from the kitchen
was smashed into floors and faces, and beer bottles were thrown

from the balcony onto the street. Pandemonium took hold of all the boys and some of the girls. I saw one of my close friends, a 6-foot 7-inch guitar player, fall onto the ground and start go into seizure, the needle still in his huge, muscled arm. It took four or five friends to pin him down. Things started to feel dangerous, so I decided to take off with Stella and the new wave girls who were leaving to go dance at the gay bar that let underage punk and new wave kids in.

The gay bar was its own scene. All the gay boys were dressed for the holidays and dancing to Soft Cell, Wire and Joy Division. We took small hits of blotter and got on the dance floor and spun each other around, flouncing with the boys until the early hours of the morning, with the twinkling lights ever more festive.

After the macho wildness of the after-party at Apartment 66, it was relatively wholesome for us to be there. We could be affectionate and not have to worry about being terrorized by guys. These guys wanted us to be there, but they didn't want to leave with us or make us feel afraid. Most of the bars in Vegas would stay open all night, so when the sun came up and every-one started to leave to go to bed, Stella and I left to go home and sleep. We didn't realize until we left the club at dawn that we had parked in a no-parking zone, and that the car had been towed hours before.

We sat on the curb in the parking lot trying to figure out who to call. We were miles too far to walk and, in our 50s thrift store pumps, wouldn't have made it far on foot anyway. It was then that I noticed someone sitting in a late 70s muscle car across from us, watching. He had a weathered face, and he looked familiar. In my exhausted state, I almost recognized him. He gave me a dark feeling of dread and recall that I could not yet place and did not want to place.

Stella called someone from the payphone in front of the liquor store next to the bar who she thought would take us to the tow yard and bail out her car. Her friend came and got us and drove us over there, and the elderly man in charge stared at us in our torn fishnets, 50s cocktail dresses and smeared makeup and shook his head. He took our money and handed us the keys.

Chapter 13
Right is Wrong

When things feel too grim with Todd or Jenny, there's a large hotel that caught fire in 1980 that I like to visit. I try to find hotels to ride to all the time to distract myself and, when I can't, I go looking for spirits who can see me. This one is filled with the half-charred, smoke-choked ghosts of the people who died gambling, sleeping, drinking or trying to escape. It is lively. There are groups of specters wandering the casino floor, restrooms, stairwells and hallways. There is a sense of panic there but also a vivid sense of time and place, and most have no idea that anything is amiss.

They are from an era that I can recall, and I feel very comfortable in their presence. It is as if I am alive again when I am there. I also like to visit a hotel my father worked at when I was a child, the International, that eventually became the Hilton. I see the ghost of a handsome dark-haired man in a sparkling white suit, a giant belt buckle and an embellished cape. He stands near the showroom and sometimes near the service elevator. I have a ghost crush on this spirit who feels so familiar, so I loiter in the green room where he appears smiling, winking, sexy and charismatic. He sometimes wears sunglasses, often he has on a scarf and a big belt. I notice the belt is embellished with an E, and it reminds me of my family. Sometimes he sees me and winks at me and flirts a little and says, "taking care of business in a flash."

I visit the Tivoli Gardens restaurant to watch the ghost of a flamboyant bachelor piano player, drinking from a goblet with handsome young male companions who look just like him. He sometimes plays ghost piano for us. I visit the Circus Circus where I watch a teenage ghost girl write *HELP ME* in lipstick on the mirror in the downstairs bathroom near the poker room. I follow her up to her hotel room where she's being kept by the ghost of an older man. They both have strangulation indents in their necks. She lies prone on the bed and looks to me to be forever awaiting customers. I often follow a woman down a hallway into a room where the body of her child is on the floor with a gunshot wound. The woman shoots herself in the head, then returns to wander the hallways.

I lurk in the Flamingo Hotel, where the spirit of an ambitious and violent man in a fine suit sits near the pool in a robe or waits for someone in the wedding chapel. His suit is riddled with bulletholes, and he's got one smashed up eye socket, and he's always demanding things from people who cannot see him. He behaves like an emperor. He is frequently noticed by the living because he's always trying to command them. If he sees me, he hisses, bangs, sings and snarls. Sometimes he shouts at me "kill her!" or "you broke in here!"

Sometimes he appears with a glamorous woman wearing oversized sunglasses. She's slender and elegant but does not seem attached to the hotel the way he does.

I find distraction and exhilaration in these places, but I never find my way out of death, and no one I meet knows the way home.

Chapter 14
I'm Not the One

Deathly bored of the stalking hotels again, so my mind returns to the tow yard, where I left with my friend Stella in her car after the winter night in the gay bar. As we left, I noticed the Charger from the liquor store where we used the payphone following behind us. The man driving it had a beard, mustache and sunglasses. He was wearing a leather vest and, when I saw it, I felt something disgusting pass through me. He followed us back to Stella's house. I was terrified, but I said nothing to Stella. When we arrived at her home where her parents were still sleeping, and we parked in the driveway, he slowed down and removed his sunglasses and leered at us.

I again said nothing because Stella had noticed nothing. Both of us were exhausted from the all-night-dancing-tow-yard ordeal and, as we walked toward the house, we wondered aloud if her parents were awake and would find us as we snuck back in.

She had left her bedroom window unlocked, so we climbed over the fence and into her room. We snaked off all the night's leather regalia onto the floor, pulled on our ubiquitous sleepwear – oversized threadbare band t-shirts: hers said The Cramps, mine said The Flesh Eaters, and we climbed into bed. After a moment, she slipped into the hallway bathroom to pee. She came back in and whispered that they were still asleep. We smiled at how lucky we were to not be caught. She quietly put on a record, and we fell asleep. I could hear the sound of a car engine revving outside as I drifted off into a nauseous slumber.

When her parents woke us up an hour or so later, her dad was angry. He called us into the living room, and he asked us about the man who knocked at the door, asking for me. I feigned ignorance, and Stella was believable in her lack of knowledge about who he could have possibly been. Her father asked why the man asked for me. I said nothing and stared at the shag carpet or the macrame owl on the wall.

Stella, always quick of mind and feet, told her dad that we were supposed to go out for breakfast with Jessie, as a way to get out of the house immediately and make it seem like we were rested and had a morning game plan. Her dad's anger was intense, and we needed an escape. Thank you, Stella, I thought. We got dressed in warm clothes and got back in her car as her mom tried to calm her dad down. There was no Charger on the street but, as we rounded the corner, it was there and started up and tailed us again as we headed downtown. I had no idea what to do and again was mute. Stella asked if I wanted to go get the dollar breakfast at the Fremont hotel. I mumbled a yes while checking to see if I had a dollar and change, and we drove there and parked, and so did the Charger.

We silently entered the casino through the back by the pool, and the man got out and followed us. One of our older friends, Z, worked the day shift in the casino hair salon, and Stella mentioned on the way in that maybe we could borrow the keys to his apartment to be able to go sleep some more. We found him on our way in, and he said, "Hell, yes, honey" to her request. We ordered and quickly ate some scrambled eggs, hash browns and buttered toast with jelly, and then headed back out to the parking lot to drive to Z's place, which was close by.

The man in the Charger did nothing to hide the fact that he was following us, but I just abruptly stopped thinking about it. I became resigned, a freeze response taking shape in my guts, the magic from the night before turning into the inability to feel anything, even fear. The initial fight or flight response I first had at the sight of him in the car turned into a determined resignation to face whatever was in store for me. I wasn't planning to submit to him, but I also had no strategy because I was stuck like a deer in the headlights.

After we arrived at Z's place, we climbed up bouncy metal and concrete steps to the second floor of the 60s style apartment. When we got inside, the heater was on, and the warmth and quiet and nice wood floors made us both super sleepy. Stella went and crashed in Z's bed and, listening as footsteps passed by the doorway a few times, I passed out on the couch in the living room, filled with breakfast and dread.

Chapter 15
My Life's a Waste

I ghost stalk Jenny again. She's back with the man I found her with at the motel a few nights before. They are scoring meth from the bartender at the Blue Angel motel bar near Boulder Highway. I follow them back to the room they are renting at a decrepit Single Room Occupancy on Fremont. I watch as they prepare some foil and a straw-sized pipe and smoke up drugs into hazy vaporous clouds. They smile at each other, giddy, and the man proceeds to have violent sex with motionless Jenny on the floor. I refuse to watch. The oddly creepy and familiar man finishes as the phone rings. He answers, coughs out a crusty laugh, and says into the receiver, "Hell, yes, come on over."

When the visitor arrives to fuck Jenny for money, Jenny's eerily familiar boyfriend leaves and goes to smoke out in the parking lot. I notice his face on the way out. He's craggy and worn and missing a few teeth. He's wearing clothes sized for a man who eats three meals a day, but they are hanging off his stringy frame. He has gray facial hair and a bald head and a saggy leather vest, one with a patch on the back that gives me an instant and horrible flashback to when I was alive.

Suddenly my ghost mind is back at Z's apartment, waking up to the sound of the phone ringing. The phone rings for a long time, stops, then rings again for a long time. Stella finally answers the extension next to the bed. I hear her say, "Z's house, Stella speaking…yeah, sure… Z won't mind." Then the sound of the ding of the receiver as it lands on the princess phone body when she hangs up. The bedroom door opens, and the bathroom door closes. She takes a long shower while I stare blankly at the glittery popcorn ceiling.

A half an hour later, a bunch of our friends from the gig and party the night before arrive, looking for a place to do drugs and continue after the friends who live at Apartment 66 kicked everyone out so they could sleep. It is dusk, which means I had slept for at least 6 hours, but I was groggy, and I had lost track of time. Z's apartment was a notorious place to get high and frolic, and I had been to these impromptu Z's place-drinking-fests a couple of times before, usually leaving before the drugs began. The real holiday party had already started the previous night at the gig, and Todd was with the group that arrived with more drugs, and it was clear he had not slept at all.

I was still on the couch wrapped in a blanket when they came inside, and Stella was doing her hair in the bathroom. Todd sat on the couch next to me and put his hands up under my shirt, saying that he needed to warm them up. His knife-cold touch was shocking and welcome, but I wasn't able to respond. He handed me a beer, and I drank it, glad to have an aspirin to pour into my unresponsive body, to maybe thaw my soul. The second wave of guests arrived after Z got home from work, and they had hard liquor, but all the drugs were gone.

Someone called their drug dealer. I drank another beer with Todd and watched the antics. There were sticky Knox-gelatined upright hairstyles that had fallen down and were dripping white crispy goo on the faces from the gig the night before. Couples were forming out of the detritus of multiple combinations of drugs. There were boys with boys and girls with girls and all the other bodily combinations. People were watching cartoons and laughing at the stupid violence. The music on the record player was The Psychedelic Furs, as Z's taste was more new wave than punk. "Sister of mine, home again…" was coming from the record player, and a sax part repeated. I liked the feeling of being a little less sober than usual, and I let it relax me into Todd's arms, and quickly we were making out on the couch.

Soon the drug dealers arrived. I was in a tipsy embrace under the blanket, when I looked up to see a surreal scene, The Charger-driving stalker from the mansion party glancing at me repeatedly while selling heroin to a girl with smeared eye makeup. He said loudly that he had acid, and a couple of people bought it, splitting the cost of a quarter of a sheet of blotter. I tried to ignore him, but he was unable to stop staring at me. In my beer buzz, I was brash and not afraid, and so I stared at him defiantly and told Todd loudly that that guy was an asshole and scammer of the highest order of scammers and assholes, and then I turned my head away and very obviously ignored him. I wasn't much of a drinker, so it's no surprise that somehow I was suddenly much more interested in making out with Todd than anything else.

Chapter 16
Someday

Visiting Todd's house, I watch him make dinner for his son,
as his ex has allowed visitation occasionally. He's sweating
from last night's binge, and I'm listening to the silent serenity
prayer he's repeating in his head from the meeting he went to
before he picked up his kid. The boy is watching television in
the adjacent living room and seems happy to be with his dad.
They are talking over the TV, and I find the conversation so
mundane and lovely I wish I could cry. But I can't cry, because
I don't exist.

Todd senses me near him and immediately flashes to the
night of the party at Z's when he convinced me to do acid with
him. Standing at the stove cooking a steak, he reminisces about
that evening, when he got to the party and how I was wrapped
in a blanket on the couch, how he was able to get me a little
buzzed and remembers how that made me more susceptible to
doing drugs with him, something I normally refused to do.
He remembers how he took the blotter from the sheet and put
the tab on my tongue, closing my mouth and kissing me. He
remembers how, a while after the kissing, I pushed him away

and started laughing and refused to have sex with him when he tried, that I wanted to lie on the floor under the plants that were suddenly more alive than the people, breathing by the window, and to talk and listen to records.

He remembers that we talked about the future and where I was going to move to once I graduated high school. I had been to San Francisco when I was twelve and decided to move there during that visit. I was telling him about wandering around Chinatown with a friend and how we bought a newspaper that featured a headline about piles of dead bodies in a place called Jonestown, people in a cult that had died from drinking poisoned Kool-Aid. I often said that San Francisco was beautiful and surrounded by ocean and that he would love it and had to move there with me, and he winces as he recalls that I said once again that I was going to *get the fuck out of Vegas someday.*

He recalls that after the party had died down, the creepy drug dealer was sitting at the dining table watching us as we laid on the floor talking and laughing under the potted plants, me staring at the leaves and telling him they were pumping blue-red plant blood through their veins just like humans do while he laughed, and how we watched a rubber skeleton hanging from one of the macrame planters as it did a macabre dance just for us. Todd remembers standing up and telling the drug dealer, who just sat down at the kitchen table staring at me, to leave. The drug dealer said, "No, I'm not leaving." Todd remembers wandering off into the bathroom, finding Maxine in there doing a line and, that after Maxine closed the door and he took a leak, that she blew him. He remembers the acid getting stronger and forgetting about me and leaving the bathroom with Maxine, finding the smaller bedroom open when Z's bedroom was not, and how they went in and shut the door. Then he slips back to the present and notices he's burning his son's steak, stops the reverie, and calls his son into the kitchen to set the table.

Chapter 17
Half Skull

I suddenly fly from Todd to Jenny. She is resting on a broken bed in a broken room, and her pimp is next to her on the bed. I reach out so that he can feel the clammy hand of his own hubris and denial as it grabs his balls and pulls him under to where I'm waiting for him, down in the void. I feel a wake of anger and malignant narcissism from him and the smell of the lingering air of bad body odor at the racetrack when it's being swept. He smells like the smell of burning rags and of chlorine at a summer pool, mixed in with the scent of decaying lilies at a funeral.

I realize that I have had this stench on me twice before, once when I woke up at the party mansion, and also the night when my body was dropped into the dirt out by Lake Mead. I remember that I was buried with this death-scent on me, while I was still breathing. I see that his home is the rent-by-the-hour SRO where I have visited Jenny before. I stand over him as he lies on the bed, wracked by withdrawals, not yet in the vomiting and shitting stage. He's cold and the sheets are soaked with the fluids of a man swimming in sulfur. His sallow skin is sagging on the hollows of his skull, and his vampiric eyes peer out like withered prunes in a bowl of milk.

He can see me and remembers singling me out at his old boss' party to give me the drink with the drugs in it. He remembers playing with my body like a rag doll in the basement of the party, doing whatever he wanted to it, and the memory of that violence has him reaching by reflex down to grab his flaccid junk, which he tugs weakly. It won't respond, and he fills with vitriol and rage. He stares at my ghost face and screams obscenities at me. I watch him closely until he swipes his weak arms up to try to hit me.

I slink up to the ceiling, where I cling to acoustic tiles and watch breath oozing out of him like a black vapor. I look into the black hole of his mind and see his memories of his alcoholic father, a proud member of the KKK, who beat him mercilessly, and his sadistic stepmother who put out her cigarettes on him before having him perform sex acts on her. I understand that there is the bleak absence of a soul in him, an emptiness formed in a dank and violent belly of a beast of white supremacy, domestic and sexual violence.

His choice was to become just like them and like all the ancestors before them. I see the lineage of his people going back into the centuries of American depravity, where violent and racist whiteness was celebrated and child rape was a family tradition. His carrying on the family traditions started with him doing his dad's drugs and alcohol before he was old enough to drive a car. He learned how to drive in order to sell drugs to his classmates for his father, and to pimp out hitchhiking women from his childhood bedroom, women that he picked up for his father on the outskirts of town. The small office room in their dilapidated house out by Smoke Ranch Road was filled with guns and ammunition, stockpiled for the coming race war. I can see the skeleton bodies of the hitchhiking girls they buried out in the desert off Smoke Ranch Road in his mind.

Chapter 18
Turning Into What You Hate

Later, I watch as a man finishes fucking Jenny in the broken room on the broken bed of the same SRO and then punches her in the stomach while she is lying naked and thin as the lamp post outside, the one with the dull light. She doubles up in pain, winces and cries out, but there are no tears. I think maybe she can't cry, the same as me.

The man leaves the room and pays Jenny's pimp $40 in the parking lot on his way to his car. Her pimp goes back upstairs to the room in the SRO, sits on the bed with a barely noticeable bulge and looks at Jenny. Jenny tries to smile at him, and I see the face of the girl she had been with me; innocent, tender, desperately wanting to be loved. The pimp boyfriend leers at her, takes off his leather vest and tosses it on the floor. He unbuckles his jeans and shoves his half- erection into her mouth, moving roughly against her face while she chokes and gags with his awkward thrusts. That seems to arouse him more, so he becomes even rougher with her, smashing the sides of her head clumsily with his stupid hands. I look away, listening to the sickly moaning of him finishing, sounding like a man dying of an incurable disease. Jenny lies on the bed barely breathing. I notice the patch on the back of the leather vest as it lay on the floor.

Staring at the patch, suddenly I slip into the time and place when Jenny and I stood by the Zipper ride, after the man with the disguised voice hopped off, rushing away that night at the Helldorado fair. How, after I climbed out, my body shook as if I was standing naked in the snow. My carnival-going friends laughed at me at first, as I stood there shuddering, but then Jenny noticed it wasn't a joke.

I remember how she came up to me and silently put her arms around me and held me. The embrace and her kindness brought me down from the place outside my body, the place I had climbed to since the night at the party mansion. Standing there, with the mechanical loudness and the sounds of people screaming on the rides, I could hear her faint breathing. I felt myself starting to breathe with her, and soon I was back in my own head and body in front of the Zipper. I loved her.

Now I'm looking at the weathered vest patch on the floor of the SRO, the one embellished with the logo of a motorcycle gang. I remember the patch on the vest of the man exiting the ride at the carnival. I stare at his malevolent smile, the one that followed Stella's car and found me at Zs apartment that night. The same weak body of the man who was once also my stalker and then my killer. I swoop myself over Jenny, covering her live body with my not-body, silently ushering her to the place she took me that time before, standing outside the Zipper ride at the Helldorado fair.

I hold her with all my will, my thin veil of my energy encircling her, attempting to provide the same warmth she once gave to me. "Mick, Mick is that you?" she asks aloud, quietly. The murderer-pimp startles us both: "What the fuck you just say, whore?" I scream out inside myself YES, JENNY IT'S ME! She hears me, she prays for me to save her. "Save me!" she screams out.

The rapist pimp stares at her with a cruel smirk. He thinks she's still too high to know what's going on or what just happened to her. He pushes her head down onto the bed with his stinking hand and tells her to be quiet. I immediately leave her body and fly up to the ceiling. I rip the cheap glass lighting fixture off from over the bulb and throw it at his head, narrowly missing as he ducks with his old meth reflexes, instead hitting the wall behind him, glass shards raining all over the beat-up dresser. He stands and spins his head up toward the ceiling toward where the fixture had flown off, looking up and then looking at Jenny like he's certain she just pulled some shit, but then noticing there's no way she could have attempted that at the angle the fixture flew from to where it broke apart.

She curls up in a fetal position with a pillow over her head, smiling. I want to hurt him badly, but there's nothing in the room I can do any real damage with, mostly because I am not alive. So I slam dresser drawers open and shut, I turn the sad faucet in the room sink on full blast, I take his keys and throw them at the medicine cabinet above the sink. The mirror doesn't break, but I am loud.

Jenny is hiding her face, almost laughing. I bang on the dresser, pick up the larger glass shards and smash them violently into smaller bits. I take the $40 out of his vest pocket and light it on fire, using his lighter by standing it on the dresser and willing it to light. I love that I can make fire, the fury of my anger becoming a portal between time and space. He stares at the burning, floating money and thinks that the drugs they smoked were maybe laced with PCP.

He shivers at the feeling of cold hate I surround him with, takes a tiny bag of heroin out of his pants pocket while I continue to bang about, and I toss a shower of the ashes of the money on to him. He smokes from tinfoil, until he passes out in a fog next to Jenny. Jenny lets out a giggle under the pillow as she falls asleep, high as a kite, thinking of me, of carnival rides, of our friendship.

Chapter 19
Buried Alive

Suddenly my mind is back at the party, and Todd has gone into the bedroom with Maxine, and I am in the living room high on LSD and unaware of my surroundings. The drug dealer is standing over me as I lie under the plants, no longer listening to new wave music, just the quiet of the end of the party, the lovers who have left and are in the bedrooms or on couches.

I am staring up at his face as it blends and morphs into the faces of cartoon characters I had seen on the television earlier. I don't see his face, I see a cartoon cat, then a cartoon mouse, then a cartoon ham and then a cartoon fist. He has a blue bandana in his hand. He pushes it over my mouth and nose, and I try to breathe, but there is a strong smell and a sweet taste in my mouth, and then I am not anywhere anymore.

I wake up lying face down in the corner of a strange room on burgundy shag carpeting, no longer at Z's place. I am bound, hands behind my back and my feet together, with duct tape. I am naked and bleeding from my scalp and from my mouth onto the duct tape that is over my lips. The blood is filling up my mouth but leaking out and separating the duct tape from my skin. I move my tongue, and there are teeth loose in my mouth.

The shag carpeting underneath me is wet. I lift my head a little. I feel all the blood beneath me. I notice the blood is pooling from me, from between my legs, I can feel it there, dark and wet. I can't see my body, I just know the feeling of the wetness of the blood underneath me. The pain is there in a dull, everywhere way.

My eyes take in the fake oak wood paneling on the walls, and I hear someone stirring behind me. I hear the sound of a shotgun being cocked. Something is placed against the back of my head. A loud sound, a smashing of all the things in my head, and then it's dead quiet.

I fly up to the ceiling, out to the roof, into the night sky and out past the lights of the city, to look at the stars from the darkest place I can find in the desert night. I see Venus, I see Mars, I see lunar craters. I see coyotes running on the earth below. I see night blossoms opening. I see the beginning and end of my time. And then I am back on the ground, being dropped into my grave, dirt being tossed from a shovel onto my sheet-covered body, still bleeding out, still breathing shallowly through the blood.

Chapter 20
I Can't Take it No More

I am standing invisibly next to Jenny as she struts in front of the SRO wearing a long t-shirt, beat up thigh-high pleather boots, dirty underwear and no pants. She is bruised, and open sores are visible on her arms and thighs. She is advertising her body at dusk in the cold, her pimp looking down at her from the window on the second floor. She's trying to pose in a seductive way, hiding the tracks and abscesses and attempting not to notice the temperature. Cars pass and, if one stops, she will usually negotiate for a minute before getting in. Tonight she's unlucky, and no one stops. She's run out of makeup, and it's hard to disguise the bruises on her face, arms and legs.

When she finally slumps and heads back up the stairs to the room, her pimp greets her with yet another nasty request for drug money. She looks down at the floor, littered with dirty spoons, tinfoil and used needles. He searches her body and boots, finds nothing and proceeds to beat her again. I see him from behind as he slaps her face viciously, whips off his belt and strikes her on the side where he thinks the strap welts will be hidden by her hair.

My eyes are frozen on the patch of his droopy vest, the one that advertises his old motorcycle gang affiliations. I know him from the blood I let out on the burgundy shag carpeting, I know his sick energy, I know that his DNA was in me when I was placed in my grave, and I know he is going to kill her, too.

I float out to the front of the SRO and use the receiver on the payphone and will it to call Jenny's mother, having memorized their home phone number in middle school. My electricity and rage crackles and hums through the line, and Jenny's mom picks up before she hears the phone ring. Jenny's mom hears a disembodied voice repeat the words *SAVE HER* and the address of the SRO. She asks loudly, "Save who?" I scream *JENNY! SAVE HER!* She hears me somehow through the loud portal scratches on the telephone line and writes the address down on a notepad next to her bedside. She calls the police and drives to the address she has written down.

I return to the hotel room and force my spirit into an apparition of who I was the night I died. My body is young and alive again, I am filled with water and not with dust, and my skin is warm and soft. I am dressed in the same clean t-shirt and fishnet tights I slept in on Z's couch right before I died, and I am floating up the stairs like an angelic drug mule, holding bags of ghost cocaine, meth, heroin and needles in my phantom hands. Jenny is lying beaten and unconscious on the floor, alive but barely breathing. He sees me appear at the doorway. I am a beacon, and the desire for what I am and what I am holding out to him wells up in his desiccated mind and body. He stands, puts on his vest like an automaton and follows me outside, completely enchanted.

I float backwards, facing him, looking into his hollow eyes, down the stairs while offering heaven in my hands. I entice him out onto the street where the men drive by, trolling for sex workers. I wait until a semi-truck carrying a load of new Cadillac El Dorados is visible a block away. I step into the street, beckoning him to follow me. He steps off the curb, into my hallucinatory embrace. I stand motionless as the semi smashes into him and the wheels destroy his body, the driver hits the brakes violently, and I then I gaze over him, looking down at his mangled corpse, the vest covered with his gore.

The police arrive and find him, a pulp of flesh on the street, with the truck driver stopped a few yards away, shaking at the wheel. I watch as they light the flares and block off the crime scene. The SRO manager joins them in the street. After a discussion about the accident, where he explains that he saw him walking by himself out into the path of the semi, and that the driver was caught off guard, he then leads them up the stairs into the room where Jenny's body lies in collapse on the dirty floor.

Her mom parks and spots the open door and police surrounding the room, walks the stairs to the room, identifies her daughter through tears, as an ambulance is summoned. The paramedics arrive. I stand behind her mother as she cries, willing Jenny to live. The police detain Jenny's mom, questioning her as to how she knew where her daughter was after she had reported her missing a few weeks ago. She explains a strange phone call, suggests that a friend of her daughter's tipped her off. I ride with them to the hospital, watching as Jenny's coma is induced and she's put on life support.

Chapter 21
Just a Dream

Suddenly, after Jenny leaves the SRO, I am free. I am released from the attachment to my body and my friends and the living. I no longer want to visit hotels to look for the dead or explode with the dying old resorts. I go home to say goodbye to my family, the family I had all but forgotten about in the heat of my teenage passions. I go to our house, I see my dad getting ready for the night shift at the Hilton, my mom making dinner and my brothers rehearsing in the garage. I say goodbye to them. I say I'm sorry. I say it's not forever, that I will be with you always, and someday again. I visit Stella, and I hug her with my whole heart. I don't know how to tell everyone that I feel free and light as a bird, and that I'm going home to see my grandmothers. They are sad, recovering from not knowing what happened to me, and yet they are living on, learning to deal with the thought that I vanished without a trace.

Then I visit Todd, and he is lying on a bed at the Rummel in the dark of the night, half asleep. I find a package of matches next to the bed and move them to the toilet. I don't know if he's high, and I don't want him to wake up and accidentally light the place on fire.

I hover on the bed next to him. He's looking out of the corner of his eyes over at the spot where I float, not knowing if the feeling that I am there is real.

I watch him slump into a drunken sleep. He wants to forget that he left me under the plants at Z's party to go fuck Maxine in the spare bedroom, the last place anyone saw me. I want him to know that after I was gone, how I was with him right after, and with him when he did cocaine to be able to go to work, and how I watched him at work. That I would wait for him to come back to the room, hoping he would notice all the signs I'd put in place, especially the copy of *Fear and Loathing* I found in the motel dumpster and placed on the floor of his van, angry that he'd thrown it away. I wish that he knew that I was there while he tried to kill himself slowly the whole time they searched, until they decided I was a missing person and until he decided to leave that room and find someone living to love him. I was with him when he found the person that would love him and, as he hung the tin heart over his desk under the picture of his mom, I tried to force the words *I love you* into his head again and again.

In his sleep, he feels a surge of something, because I am sending the force of all of my energy out, trying to tell him that I love him. I want to make him feel it from within, the way I made Jenny feel it. I want him to let go of his ache for annihilation. I want to tell him that he did not kill me, that even though they never found my body, I am still with him, that he and Stella and my family were the first people I flew to. I want him to know I lay with him in his motel night after night, right by his side, listening to him sob and call out for his mom after she died and I was gone. I want him to know that I tried to push the words

I love you into his head night after night, hoping that he would hear the words repeated in his own voice. None of it will make any sense, I think.

And then I am gone.

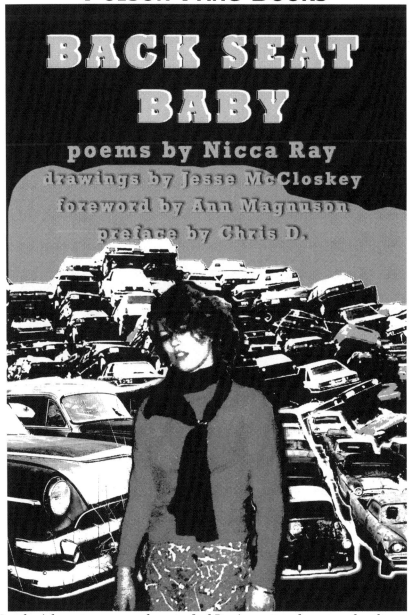

The life of recovering addict and Namvet Milo unravels when ex-CIA friend Dave goes off the deep end. Not only is Dave the heist man whacking NYC drug dealers, he's also hatching a scheme to plunder mob boss Nunzio's art treasures pilfered in WWII. Complicating matters, Yuen, an ex-Viet Cong with a grudge against Milo and Dave, arrives in New York.

"A healthy authorial sense of curiosity and generosity lends weight to No Evil Star's intersecting lives, where Chris D. ably traces out the contours of human torment in a manner recalling American films of the 1970s."
– Grace Krilanovich, author of THE ORANGE EATS CREEPS

AVAILABLE NOW FROM POISON FANG BOOKS

In Chris D.'s title novella, brilliant, alcoholic Anne, unable to succeed in downtown L.A.'s arts community, helps a Japanese-American girl escape forced prostitution, only to ignite a string of violent deaths. In "The Glider," a British policewoman falls in-love with a serial killer near the white cliffs of Dover; plus five more twisted love tales.

"...seems to shimmer with menace... with DRAGON WHEEL SPLENDOR, the great Chris D should finally find the audience he deserves...a book that can kill the voices in your head - or make you love them."
– Jerry Stahl, author of PLAINCLOTHES NAKED, PAINKILLERS and PERMANENT MIDNIGHT

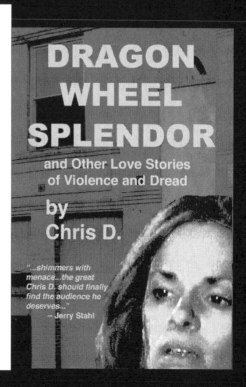

DRAGON WHEEL SPLENDOR
and Other Love Stories of Violence and Dread

by Chris D.

"...shimmers with menace...the great Chris D. should finally find the audience he deserves..."
– Jerry Stahl

The year is 1987, and outlaw Ray Diamond's mother is the queenpin of crime in Mystic, GA. After his Navy discharge, Ray knocks over a mob-connected El Paso liquor store, not counting on Eli, the owner's psycho son, dogging his trail. Back home in Mystic, Ray's girl, Connie Eustace, resorts to stripping at Mama Lorna's club to make ends meet. Witness to a murder by the local sheriff, she goes on a drug-and-drink bender, jumping from the frying pain into the fire.

"...a crazy dive into a universe populated largely by monsters...a classic update of the Gold Medal/Lion Library loser noir tradition. Great work... "
– Byron Coley, writer for WIRE magazine, author of C'EST LA GUERRE: EARLY WRITINGS 1978-1983

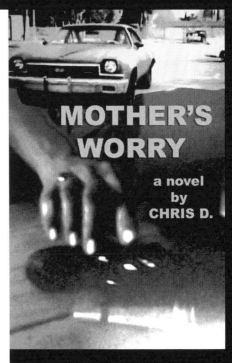

MOTHER'S WORRY

a novel
by
CHRIS D.

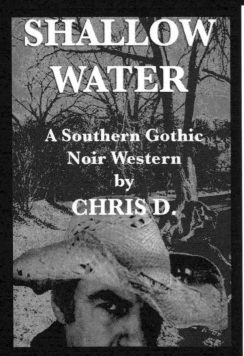

SHALLOW WATER

A Southern Gothic
Noir Western
by
CHRIS D.

Post-Civil War, bitter rebel veteran and bounty hunter, Santo Brady, drifts through the Deep South. When he rescues halfbreed Indian prostitute, Lucy Damien, from one backwater town, he has the world fall in on his head. They embark on a freight-train-hopping odyssey to New Orleans, unaware that Lucy's rich white father and homicidal brother are tracking them. A tragic tall tale plunging head-first into a wild heart of darkness.

"One sinister serpent of a story, an old Republic Pictures western serial scripted by James M. Cain and reimagined by Sam Peckinpah. I loved it."
– Eddie Muller, author of THE DISTANCE and SHADOW BOXER, host of Noir Alley on TCM

More Crime Fiction by CHRIS D.

Half-sisters, schoolteacher Mona and junkie punk rocker Terri, are uneasy roommates while taking care of their sick mother. When their boyfriends, cop Johnny Cullen and killer Merle Chambers, clash due to labor struggles in their small town of Devil's River, the two women are pulled into the fray. To make matters worse, jealous female sheriff, Billie Travers, decides Mona is intruding on her faltering love affair, and quiet small town life amps up into an apocalyptic nightmare of uncontrollable violence and destruction.

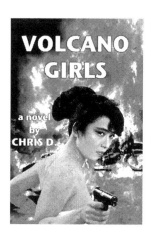

Corrupt female police detective, Frankie Powers, is treading water in her small desert hometown of Sweet Home, California. Burned-out and emotionally numb after losing her husband and child in a mysterious fire ten years before, her conscience is reawakened when her affair with a Bakersfield narc brings new facts to light. Frankie's mob boss uncle, Jack Richman, has been kidnapping under-age girls for his Vegas prostitution syndicate; he's also been victimizing his own teen daughters, Frankie's twin bad girl cousins, Valerie and Vanessa. Soon Frankie finds herself singlehand-edly fighting tooth-and-nail against not only wicked uncle Jack but also his dominatrix wife, Marilyn and their degenerate hitman, Cal Nero. Can a lone shewolf survive against the bloodthirsty pack?

from **P**oison **F**ang **B**ooks

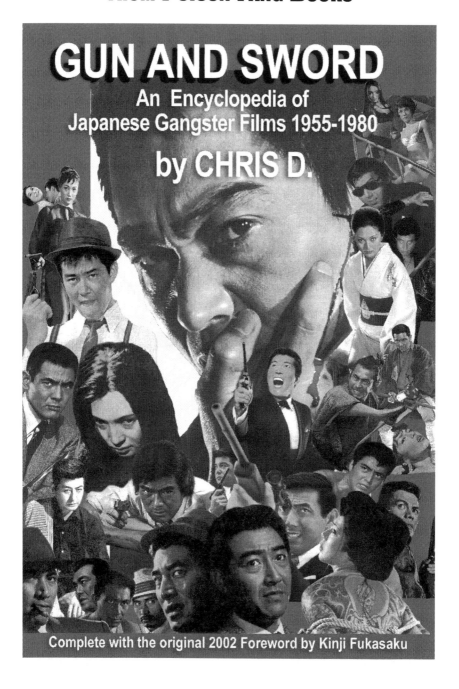

Made in the USA
Middletown, DE
21 February 2021